Sherlock Holmes

and the Eye
of Mad Bear

Also by John Elvin

the Andy Holliday mystery series:

Murder by Bay Breezes

The Never Mined Murder (Coming 2015)

Sherlock Holmes

and the Eye of Mad Bear

John Elvin

Based on the notes of Mycroft Holmes

Cover art: Martha Elvin
Cover and book design: Dean Fetzer, **www.gunboss.com**

ISBN: 978-0-9929653-3-4

Chapter One

Had I known that one day I might take it upon myself to set the record straight regarding my brother's lengthy absence from the public eye, I certainly would have saved more of the relevant notes and reference material from that time. In my line of work, though, one is advised and often required to ensure that there will be no evidence remaining.

One matter I wish to clarify concerns the arrest of Dr John Watson for murder. Do not for a moment suppose I believed him guilty of the crime. Of course, given the right circumstances, even the most respectable persons are capable of astonishing behavior. In Watson's case, strong drink had brought him near to ruin, so I suppose anything was possible. I will address the matter further as it occurs in the course of events which I am relating.

Sherlock is lately the subject of legion rumors and myths, some the result of his association with tale-spinning Dr John Watson and others the manufacture of admirers or those scheming to capitalize on his fame. I suppose I have heard or seen fifty and more stories claiming to tell the truth of his 'lost' years. All the while I have kept my peace. I will not dispute accounts of his time in Lhasa, Kabul, or venturing across Persia to the Mediterranean. I was not party to those adventures. But having played a significant role in what came after, it seems up to me to provide, to the extent I am able, an accurate account of those events. Either that or allow to stand a multitude of ridiculous myths and rumors as Sherlock's legacy.

I say *to the extent I am able* because I must rely largely upon memory. As for asking my brother or Watson to confirm details as needed, the reader will see that they have in fact contributed over the years through conversation and letter. Watson was, of course, notorious for confusion and unreliability when it came to memory, and now, as we know from tattle in the press, the poor fellow has wandered off to Afghanistan in his mind. From the porch of the home for veterans he searches imaginary hills for the Afghani whose Jezail musket caused recurring discomforts over the years. Sherlock, still able and fit, is retired to the clover-covered meadows of the Sussex Downs with his beloved bees, having taken a vow of silence with regard to past exploits.

I shall begin at the point where mystery enshrouds the whereabouts of my brother, that being in the aftermath of the confrontation at Reichenbach Falls involving Professor James Moriarty. While the world attempted to deal with news of his doom, Sherlock communicated with me via secret channels we had previously arranged.

Initially, Sherlock felt news of his survival of that epic struggle should be kept from his associate, Dr Watson, as it was being kept from the world at large. I concurred. My brother's concern was that Watson might become vulnerable to attack by Moriarty's avengers should his old friend possess information regarding his whereabouts. My own concern was for my brother's safety, having witnessed Watson's devil-may-care eagerness to rush into print with a hodge-podge of half-baked gossip about cases reaching his ears.

However, it became quite clear to me through the discreet observations of my agents that Watson, owing to the course his life had taken, was an unlikely candidate for writing anything even vaguely coherent.

Yes, sad to report, he had in his grief become something of a brain-addled sot. His life, once a merry-go-round of adventure and intrigue, was of late reduced to sitting silently in a darkened, disarrayed room, staring off at nothingness, a whiskey bottle close at hand. Callers, meaning my agents in the guise of door to door salesmen or prospective patients, reported him to be in a morbid state of mind and given to any excuse to maintain his reclusive existence.

Sometime later, Watson reflected back on those dark times in a letter to me: "My nights, as much as I could separate them from my days, were tormented by nightmare images of Holmes, teetering on the heights above the Reichenbach abyss, and then tumbling like so much debris, down and down, to be pulped on the jagged rocks at the base of that accursed chasm. The only peace or rest I knew was twilight consciousness brought on by dose upon dose of whiskey. Such was my sleep.

"As a medical man with some understanding of my own condition, I could predict it was but a matter of time until my enfeebled mind would cut loose of its moorings. Over and over, my intentions were to mend my ways, but I routinely found myself again tight as an owl and on the road to permanent delirium."

Sherlock, dodging the vengeful minions of the late Professor Moriarty, had no idea of Watson's sufferings. When, armed with considerable evidence, I informed him of the dreadful situation, he begged that I intervene. Sherlock had by that time put the remote monastery in Tibet far behind him, making his way across the forbidding far reaches of Afghanistan, finally coming to rest in the comforting warmth of the Riviera. There his dear friend, the famous stage actress and royal consort Lillie Langtry, did her best to nurse him back to health. (You may recall Mrs Langtry's appearance in one of Watson's tales as Irene Adler, though he did a fair job of disguising her with various tricks such as putting her birthplace in New Jersey, in the United States, when in fact she hails from the Isle of Jersey).

But Monaco proved unsafe after a time as Sherlock

became aware of surveillance by his pursuers, Col Sebastian Moran, heir to Moriarty's criminal web, and his ruthless henchmen. He feared his presence would put Mrs Langtry at risk. Though I assured Sherlock of the availability of safe havens in his home country, he refused. He declared that his return would quickly come to Moran's attention, and while he might be safe in hiding, Moran would come after Watson or me as having knowledge of his whereabouts. I was quite prepared to deal with the colonel should he have made an attempt on me, but Watson was as vulnerable as an abandoned infant.

I could discern from Sherlock's messages some sort of falling out between him and Mrs Langtry. My suspicion, later confirmed, was that he had jeopardized their intimacy with efforts to recover from her an artifact, an ancient amulet, which shall be discussed further on. Not that I ever suspected the relationship would blossom into romance, although I must say it revealed a side of Sherlock rarely if ever witnessed before.

So Sherlock again donned disguise and made his escape from Monaco. With feints in this direction and that, he eventually settled near an estate owned by Mrs Langtry in Saratoga Springs, in the state of New York in the United States. It seemed to me rather reckless of him to maintain proximity to Mrs Langtry, who was undoubtedly by that point being watched by Moran or his minions, but, knowing Sherlock, he had not given up on retrieval of the amulet.

At that point I received an encrypted message causing me some distress.

Chapter Two

Deciphering Sherlock's message, I discovered what I believed to be an ill-considered request. "Please send Watson to me in New York. His condition results from his belief that I am deceased; a reunion will restore him to sanity. Do not shock him with news that I am alive; I will make myself known to him when the time is right. Concoct a mission."

Easily said, but not so easily done.

There was no answer of the door when I called at Watson's residence. I knew from inquiries made by my agents that his wife, Mary, was off on a visit to her sister and had no immediate plan of return, and he had dismissed their help. Knowing his practice had dwindled to nothing, I suspected he was likely within the house but ignoring my knock. A twist of the knob provided entrance.

Following a musty odor hinting of rot, I found Watson sprawled in an easy chair in the unkempt front parlor, a drained bottle clutched to his breast as a child might cuddle a beloved toy. I tapped his shoulder with my stick, to no avail.

"Watson. Watson! Come to your senses, man."

Trembling, he squinted up at me. "Who is that?"

I am not an indistinct presence. "Mycroft Holmes. Do you not recognize me?"

Watson was beyond reach. His perplexed look told me he was lost in an alcoholic fog.

There was nothing to do but dry him out for a few days in a facility known to insiders simply as The Lodge. I am well known to the administrator and staff of that place because it has often been my duty to escort certain persons to their doors. It is not particularly unusual for senior foreign office officials to lose their grip, particularly following a field visit to some desolate or degenerate locale, and of course we do not want them going about their duties or wandering the streets until they've regained control. So we have The Lodge, a well-staffed sanitarium offering all the luxuries of a grand hotel.

In addition to the comforts there are, of course, accommodations for those requiring various levels of restraint, and burly guards at the entranceways to assure that no one leaves until officially released. For some it is but a matter of days until they are ready to go back into harness. For others it might be longer, and for a few, unfortunately, residency is permanent.

I waited while Watson was checked in. Once he had undergone an initial examination, I asked if any problem was foreseen in bringing him around.

"Not this time," the examining doctor assured me. "But he has put his brain and organs to a considerable test. Next time may see him reduced to babbling idiocy, or, perhaps the better for him, dead."

As Sherlock's companion in many adventures, Watson had often assisted in service to the Crown. It was therefore perfectly justifiable that he should be a guest of The Lodge for such time as necessary to put him right. I left my instructions: "See that he gets the best of care."

I confess that in the course of dealing with a spate of calamities and crises I rather forgot about Watson for a week or so. I will not go into the pathetic details of a note reaching me at the Diogenes Club except to say it left no question regarding his depressed state of mind. So I called at The Lodge and found him much healthier but, as his note suggested, greatly disturbed.

We met in a rotunda off the entryway, a visiting area with benches nestled among potted ferns and other large plants providing some privacy. Watson, so I was told, had created quite a ruckus at one point. He calmed down a bit when confronted by two brawny orderlies armed with a straightjacket and gag. But I suppose the sight of me caused him to again lose control.

The staff of The Lodge, by the way, was quite up to dealing with protests, dealing as they must with admirals, ambassadors, troublesome adolescents of royal blood – who are used to doing as they wish and having their wishes obeyed. To a point their tantrums were accommodated, and beyond that the staff would quite readily resort to drugs, restraints and even brute force.

Watson fumed and sputtered. "You have no right! ... Outrage! ... Illegal! ..." And on and on. He trembled as he spoke, quite possibly due to the poisonous amounts of alcohol he had previously consumed rather than as a symptom of rage.

I kept my peace, nodding along with what I hoped would be taken for a sympathetic smile. However, the Lodge staff does not long tolerate disturbances and it was the silent appearance of two orderlies that brought the harangue to a sputtering halt. After a few quiet moments Watson asked, calmly but with a distinct air of frustration, what had transpired to bring him to this place.

"It was imperative that you be shaken from the grip of, shall we say, your demon, by whatever means, because I have an important mission for you."

At that his mood turned in the direction of remorse. "You have put us both through trouble for naught, Mycroft. I am quite unfit for undertaking any sort of mission. I thank you, of course, for kindnesses shown, but now I must get back to my practice."

I'm sure my look telegraphed great skepticism. "Watson, there is no need to prevaricate regarding your situation. I have my sources. I happen to know that you are not engaged in any activity at home or at your medical offices beyond your own indulgences. Is that not so?"

He looked away from me and I continued: "Mary is off with her sister, and your practice, I dare say, consists of little more than dodging creditors."

Whatever he stared at for a few moments was not a presence in the room. Almost in a whisper he replied: "I suppose it is true."

"Suppose? You very well know it to be true. And so I have gone so far as to make necessary arrangements for your expedition."

At this, Watson hammered his knees with balled fists. "I can hardly find my way from one street corner to the next these days, Mycroft. An expedition of any sort is entirely out of the question."

"You are going to America. You will ship out next week, destined for the resort of Saratoga Springs in New York, traveling as Dr John Watkins."

He moaned and muttered and spouted further protests.

I went on as though I had heard nothing. "I am told that Saratoga Springs is a lovely place at this time of year, Watson, bustling with wealthy racing enthusiasts and not far from idyllic woodland retreats in the majestic Adirondack Mountains. The spa itself is known internationally, as I am sure you are aware, for its healing waters. As a physician, you must agree that healing waters would be of benefit in your case. Unblended, of course."

Watson shook his head. "I have read the journals, Mycroft. Hopeful visitors arrive there complaining of rheumatism, stomach trouble, nerves and all sorts of conditions, only to find that the healing qualities of the waters amount to nothing more than their purgative effect."

I was not totally in the dark about the offerings of the spa. "Perhaps you also know it is where the first temperance society in the United States was formed nearly a hundred years past, and it is currently a meeting place of the Society for Total Abstinence, a gathering where you would be most welcome, I am sure."

Watson's face colored as if he was going into a fit. "I will have no part of it and that is final. Make way, I will not be held captive!" With that, he stood and brushed aside my attempt to restrain him, raising a fist as if to deliver a blow.

Enough, thought I. Quite enough. I signaled to the orderlies. Watson sensed what was coming and made a mad dash in the direction of the front door. When last I saw him that day, he was struggling and kicking between the two orderlies like some large, freshly captured fish.

Chapter Three

Several days passed before I went again to The Lodge. (Much as I might have wished to devote greater attention to accommodating Sherlock's interests, there were matters of state, small wars, sordid scandals and such, requiring my attention at the time. Besides, the interim gave Watson time to adjust his attitude).

"Watson, there is more to this matter than I can confide to you at present. If you will but gather your courage and wits, you may come along with me to a place where we can discuss it further."

"You make it sound like a matter of state, Mycroft."

I put a hand on his shoulder, as a brace of course but with a grip sufficient to communicate my intent to steer him as I saw fit. "Come along."

We passed through the main door where my nod to the guards was sufficient to see us through to the outside. I marched Watson around the street corner. An elegant coach stood waiting.

"What is this?"

"You shall see."

The coach window curtain parted only enough to

reveal a face known to all of England. Hardly a week could pass without those hooded eyes and that close-cropped beard adorning the pages of one gossipy rag or another.

The effect was to snap Watson to military attention. I took his shoulder and turned him away, for Prince Albert Edward had agreed only to show his face; he had no wish to converse with Watson.

The Prince, I must say, took to the project with some enthusiasm. Since the days when he became the first member of the royal family to set foot in America, disguised as "Baron Renfrew," and certainly as he grew into a man of rather scandalous appetites, he found enjoyment in the clandestine adventure of one sort or another.

What brought the Prince to join in the effort to restore Watson to health?

The fact is, when I am asked to concoct a mission, I am in my element. And, to my mind, the best concoction is one rooted firmly in reality, so I set about reviewing the many problems, great and small, such as might require a mission to America. There were to be sure some of great moment, and those I dismissed for fear Watson might botch them. And there were those of such triviality that he would see through them as mere busy work. Then, almost as though it had emerged in response to this particular need, forth came a matter containing a number of intriguing and confounding elements and yet of no great consequence in the grand scheme of things.

Albert Edward – Bertie, they called him in those days, you will recall – had been among the select coterie of gentlemen involved with Sherlock's friend, the celebrated Lillie Langtry. In the course of that involvement, during which she reigned, scandalously, almost as a genuine princess, he allowed his generosity to overpower his good sense.

As it happened, a little silver trinket among the incredible treasures scattered about the royal residences caught Mrs Langtry's eye. How this particular bauble stood out, for her, in a place full of priceless gifts and tributes from all corners of the world – art, sculpture, gold, silver, jewels – I cannot guess. At any rate, Bertie rashly told her to accept it as a gift.

This trinket in question is a rather mysterious and certainly misunderstood ornament, an amulet of unusual design. It happened to have a most curious history. The amulet belonged to Sir William Johnson, an agent of the King in American colonial times who obtained it from Indian friends. They presented it upon his induction into a secret society.

As the King's agent, Johnson was closer to the Iroquois Confederacy than any white man ever, as they considered him to be a man of impeccable honesty and reliability and, in all, quite a contrast from most of the newcomers they encountered.

Sir William was told that the amulet was a badge

of membership in "The Guardians," an elite group within the Bear Clan. Supposedly, it was the duty of this group to guard a treasure housed in a secret underground chamber.

Johnson thought the subject worthy of investigation. He visited the general area described by his Indian friends but never saw the supposed treasure chamber, his trip cut short due to deteriorating health resulting from war wounds. At his death in 1774, with the American rebellion brewing, his son, who fled to Canada along with other British sympathizers, shipped a few of his cherished artifacts to the King, along with a letter explaining what little he knew of their origin. The son said he recalled his father warning in regard to the amulet that "one should avoid looking into the eye of Mad Bear," but he knew not the meaning of the phrase. Of course, the American Revolution having gone as it did, there was no subsequent investigation of the artifacts or tales related to them.

No one thought more of it; the amulet joined so many other precious treasures as a curiosity in a cabinet. A few scholars were allowed a look at it over the years. Strange though it may seem, one of them identified the piece as similar to the Hammer of Thor, worn by Viking warriors, believed to provide power and protection. This seemed an incongruous idea, but then a second scholar confirmed the identification.

This Hammer of Thor was traceable to the cult of

the Berserkers, the ferocious Viking warriors who believed they became mighty bears in battle. In ancient lore there is a tale of such an amulet which, on command, would grow to the size of a war club. A magical device, the Hammer of Thor was said to have the power to level mountains. Similar amulets have been found in many Viking gravesites and are thought to have been worn to show allegiance to Thor.

At the time it was thought that if the scholarly identification were true then Johnson's son or someone else in the chain of transfer must have mixed up the artifacts. The possibility of commerce between Vikings and Indians of the region now encompassing northern New York State was considered to be improbable, though a few dissidents, mostly amateurs, maintained otherwise. There were unreliable reports of light-skinned, blue-eyed natives in that region, a doubtful claim supporting theories of assimilation.

When I had the opportunity at a later date to examine the ornament it appeared a bit like a key of some sort, rather than being a hammer, though perhaps the shape is that of an elaborate war club or axe. It is distinctive due to the bear's head engraving, and for being made of silver, as most similar ornaments were of iron.

Chapter Four

I explained all of this to Watson as we made for my residence, where I proposed to put him up under my watchful eye pending his departure. "Unfortunately for the Prince, another scholar asked to see the amulet. It was not available, and the trail led to Bertie."

Much to my surprise, Watson seemed to have taken in some of my explanation. "Why should anyone want to hush up a simple matter of a missing trinket? Let them charge Mrs Langtry with theft of a national treasure."

"The Queen is using the issue to teach Bertie a lesson in responsibility," I replied. "Photographs of Mrs Langtry wearing the amulet have appeared in the press. Not that anyone who sees it is aware of what it is, of course."

"Not anyone?"

"Well, the Queen knew, and came close to an apoplectic fit over the matter. I hesitate to guess what price Bertie may pay if he cannot retrieve it. The Queen is so fed up with his irresponsible conduct, he might find himself in the Tower. And so he insists it must be recovered. That is your mission."

Watson stopped abruptly, turned to me and said with some vehemence: "And I insist I haven't the slightest interest in any mission, Mycroft. But I do wonder why you should even propose it?"

"Because Lillie and Sherlock were close, Watson. You know that, having alluded to it, in disguised form, in your tales."

"I know her only from biographical information assembled by your brother; information I found in his files, sandwiched between the biography of a Hebrew rabbi and that of a staff-commander who had written a monograph upon the deep-sea fishes."

"Credential enough, Watson. You are known as Sherlock's closest friend and confidante, and that should be sufficient to secure influence with Mrs Langtry. She is now in residence at her estate near Saratoga Springs, where her horses will be entered in events of the racing season – she races them under the name Mr Jersey, as women are not allowed to participate in such events."

"I read the papers, Mycroft. I know of Mrs Langtry's various connections, might I even say affairs. Certainly there are a number of powerful and influential men who could apply to her for return of the amulet. I see no sensible reason for my involvement."

I was in no mood for quibbling and my patience was wearing thin. "Come along, Watson, I will not stand here in the street debating the matter. Or would you prefer to return to The Lodge?"

We commenced our walk, though he was still greatly disturbed. "I deserve more of an explanation than you have delivered, Mycroft."

"Indeed, and I had thought to go into the thing further after dinner. Well, let me see. It is like this: Having had the utmost respect for my brother's work, the Prince has got it into his head that you will conduct yourself with similar efficiency and tact."

"I am not Sherlock Holmes."

"Point taken. But if you are unsuccessful, I fear Edward will resort to desperate measures, and that would not bode well for Mrs Langtry. He has tried bribes, he has tried threats."

Watson was having none of it. "The fact remains, despite your arguments to the contrary, I am not the man for the task. Surely there must be someone directly responsible to you who could be trusted with the mission."

Well, of course there were a dozen such and more. Further, there was a very good chance that certain of them would indeed be assigned to the mission, in that I would have them keep an eye on Watson. But it was necessary to get him on course and I determined to do so. What was needed was something to provoke fear beyond that which he felt for the journey.

"That won't do, Watson. If Edward receives the wrong answer, it could be all the worse for you."

"Meaning what, exactly?

"I would do my best to prevent such a thing from happening, but he is a man of power; he could have you clapped in lifetime solitary confinement in Bedlam or arrange that you disappear into the bowels of some wretched and remote penal colony."

On that note, we continued our walk in silence.

I am a person of the most particular routines and habits. Escorting inebriates in the throes of withdrawal is an activity far removed my usual agenda, as is entertaining visitors in my home. I am social only to the extent of having co-founded the Diogenes Club, the whole point of that organization being to provide a sanctuary for, to quote Sherlock, "the most unsociable and unclubable men in town." Typically, I would drop in at the Diogenes for a bit of peace and quiet prior to heading home for dinner. But, given his condition, I could not even trust Watson to visit the Stranger's Room at the club.

I had no reason to suspect that we might be followed at that point, but, just to be certain, I took a circuitous route to my residence, with many a glance over my shoulder. We arrived at near the dinner hour. Unlike colleagues who have small armies of staff to tend to their domestic needs, I make do with a cook and a housekeeper. My table will accommodate only six, and five of those chairs are invariably vacant.

Watson made an appreciative remark about the meal, which I let hang in the air without reply. I am a man who enjoys my meal and I do not care to have it interrupted by idle chatter. There were grilled sole, lamb cutlets, a small roast of beef and Bordeaux pigeons to be dealt with, in addition to the soup, various vegetables and finally plum pudding. While I ate with my usual vigor, Watson only nibbled and tasted, having, I suppose, the alcohol addict's intolerance for hearty meals. He was still experiencing tremors and spilled half of what he did attempt to eat.

Much as I might have enjoyed a brandy when we retired to the library, I made do with coffee and a cigar. My guest lit his pipe and studied the volumes in my bookcases. Unlike the faddists of the era who filled a room with curios, paintings and photographs and called it a library, mine actually contained a solid array of books.

In the interest of Watson's safety I broached the possibility of a slight element of danger involved in his journey. "You are aware that Moriarty had an accomplice in the ambush at Reichenbach Falls?"

Watson shook his head. "No, there was no indication of that in any report I saw. The note found at the Falls mentioned only Moriarty."

"We know with certainty that Moriarty traveled there with a companion by the name of Moran. Do you know of him?"

"The name is not familiar to me."

"Col Sebastian Moran. Nefarious sort, though the

public hasn't a clue about that. He is the new commander of Moriarty's sinister operations, a scoundrel in many ways worse than his mentor due to his appetite for murder.

"His public reputation is that of a big game hunter. Some hunt to harvest but with Moran it is only for the kill. And ultimately the hunt held too many constraints for his savage appetites, Watson. Thus was he called to crime, his specialty being assassination."

I went on to explain how Moran was rebuilding the web of criminal activity presided over by his mentor, a far-reaching network very nearly destroyed through the efforts of my brother, Sherlock.

"His influence is evident but the man himself has proven elusive," I said. "Our agents have been on alert for a sign of him for some time now, from Sebastopol to Santiago. We now believe him to be in hiding in Saratoga Springs, and I can only guess it has to do with the amulet. He must consider that its capture will provide some sort of grip on the Prince. Or it could be Moriarty left a clue as to its use as a key to a treasure. As you can see, the situation is both delicate and serious."

As had become a near habit, Watson shook his head. "I am no match for the sort of fiend you describe, particularly in my present condition. From what you say, Mycroft, the detective work is done. You know Moran's whereabouts. All you need do is have your agents lay hands on him."

"If I am not mistaken, Watson, I said we believe him to be there. He is like a shadow in a dark room; if such a thing could be, he is invisible."

Hand to chin, Watson pondered. "A shadow, of course, requires a light source."

"Good, Watson, good. You have noticed a truth about shadows. However, this particular shadow is an anomaly, thriving in the dark. Quite likely he is in disguise and using an assumed name."

I had to congratulate myself as a light of interest shown in his eyes. "Then, in the rare event such opportunity arises, how in the world will I identify him?"

"You must simply remain soberly alert, that is the idea. I recall Sherlock's comment that you *see* but do not *observe*, but in this situation your security will depend upon alertness. Do not revert to behaviors that will blind you to danger. Keep a watchful eye."

"Suppose I encounter this fellow Moran. Do you expect me to capture him?"

"Do not concern yourself with his capture; not to cast your capabilities in a bad light, Watson, but I fear he is more devil than you can handle. Alert me, and I will make a force of men available when the time comes. Your mission is to secure the amulet before he strikes."

Chapter Five

I must admit to some trepidation in regard to placing Watson aboard the ocean liner bound for New York. There was no telling what sort of villains might lurk among the 2,500 other passengers or 800 members of the crew, not to mention the temptation of the ship's saloons. But fortunately there was a man from the Foreign Office with business at the liner's destination. I asked that he keep a watchful eye on passenger Watson. As it turned out, this was no simple task.

From the first, Watson appeared to experience considerable psychic distress during the crossing, not in the least because I had made it clear to the ship's officers that he was not to be served any strong drink. According to my informant, the doctor spent the nearly seven days roaming the ship, up, down and around the various decks from what we used to call steerage, now third class, to those decks serving passengers in the majestic staterooms. It was, in fact, in one of those staterooms that Watson was accommodated, though in his restlessness he visited it only for sleep. The peripatetic wanderer looked in at the saloons, lounges, party rooms, libraries, music room and even the engine room with its roaring boilers, as well as the galley where chefs prepared meals from the larder including tons upon tons of meat and thousands of pounds of potatoes, to name but a few contents of the enormous heaps of foodstuffs making up the menus, stopping only in the smoking rooms.

At dinner he did seem to take some comfort in entertainment by the ship's small orchestra, perhaps because his shakes could be timed to the rhythm of the music, and he would pause to listen in the evenings when the musical entertainment moved to the first class deck.

"His agitation increased as the days passed," my informant wrote. "I learned that he had requested brandy from a steward who informed him of the prohibition. The only time I was forced to reveal myself was when I spotted Watson in whispered conversation with a fireman from the boiler room. As I suspected he was attempting to obtain whiskey, I interceded, much to his chagrin, and accepted the apologies of the fireman, a foreigner with little English at his command. I informed Watson that I was acting on your behalf, regretting the necessity of identifying myself as I would not, I supposed, henceforth be able to follow him incognito. That was not the case, however, as he slipped further into a mental fog, taking little notice of those around him. After that incident with the fireman, it seemed Watson's condition further deteriorated, to where he moved about in a modified St. Vitus Dance, jerking and trembling. But despite my concern, reflecting your own, it was necessary for me to part company with him at the dock, owing to pressing business on behalf of the Crown."

I should have assigned someone to permanent watch. As I was to learn in short order, Watson decided to self-prescribe for his agitation. One drink was his intention. But for a person in the grip of the alcohol demon, there is no such thing as one drink; the one is but a gateway to a destructive episode.

And so went his experience as a newcomer to New York City. Before long he was besotted again, stumbling about in a section known as the Bowery, a gloomy section of the city known for cheap saloons, vagrancy, and wanton entertainments. Among the few documents surviving from that era is a letter I received regarding Watson's situation:

My Dear Sir:

I write concerning a gentleman, or so I take him to be, recently found where he had fallen in Bowery muck, who claims your friendship and goodwill. While his papers identify him as Dr John Watkins, this person alleges that he is Dr John Watson of London, and asserts that he should be recognized as the chronicler of the adventures of your late brother, Sherlock Holmes.

As best I can determine, Dr Watson (assuming that is his name) experienced a troublesome voyage across the Atlantic, during which he suffered delirium and other debilitating symptoms of alcohol withdrawal. Then, at the conclusion of the voyage and feeling somewhat desperate, he thought he might brace himself with one small drink of whiskey. This activity proved his undoing, as persons so inclined typically proceed with their indulgence until they arrive at stupefaction. That state describes the condition in which we found your friend, if, as he asserts, he is indeed your friend. Disheveled and delirious, he was put aboard the wagon and brought to our Mission.

In due course, given Dr Watson's cooperation, he will likely emerge from his current state of confusion and provide a more coherent account. He claims a vague recollection of having been fallen upon by thugs who relieved him of his funds. This could quite well be the truth, as stealing from those in a stupor is a way of life in the quarter where he was found.

In our work we do encounter quite a few desperate rogues and imposters, and if this happens to be the case please forgive the intrusion of this letter. On the other hand, there also tend to be any number of formerly upright and prominent citizens whose downward paths we cross in our morning rescue excursions into the dismal environs they now inhabit.

While awaiting word from you we shall look after Dr Watson as best we can. He is but one among many who need our attention. It did seem this morning that his tremors were beginning to subside, though not to a point where he can conduct his own correspondence.

In the hope that you will join in our prayers seeking relief for not only Dr Watson but all who share his malady, I am

Very Truly Yours,

Maud Ballington Booth

Volunteers of America

Of course I knew of Mrs Booth and her works from newspaper accounts, including, with her husband, the recent founding of Volunteers upon their having been ousted as representatives of the Salvation Army in the United States. Despite certain controversies, she is highly regarded as an advocate for the downtrodden. So, despite this discouraging turn of events, there was some reassurance in knowing that Watson was in good hands and might yet be reformed.

As it turned out, Moran's agents must have been keeping closer eyes on Watson than were my own. The next message I received told of a close brush with doom. Much to my relief, I must say, the writing was in Watson's own hand and it was relatively steady:

> *My Dear Mycroft,*
>
> *I write to implore you to provide the wherewithal that I may quickly continue my journey and leave this wicked city behind. I have survived a second unfortunate experience since arriving here. The temptation is great to abandon my mission and return to the safety of my native shores, however, I have made my commitment and, if means are forthcoming, I shall get on with it.*
>
> *As to the most recent debacle:*
>
> *Were it not for my disoriented condition at the time I do not believe I would have*

left the Volunteers shelter in the company of the two men who called claiming to be escorts acting at your request. Much to her credit, Mrs Maud Booth pulled me aside and insisted that they hardly looked like agents of the Crown. She is quite observant and pointed out several incongruities. The one wore a bruised and dented bowler that looked as though it had taken its own course through several violent windstorms. The other's coat was frayed at collar and cuffs. Neither wore shoes of the quality one would expect of agents of the Foreign Office.

I should have taken heed. I suppose in my state I could not imagine Moran being so clever as to have learned of my connection with you and my whereabouts. I was to seriously regret my lack of respect for his evil genius.

Although my companions assured me that our carriage was 'just around the corner', the signs were otherwise. We made our way along crowded Bowery streets, jostling through milling loafers and idlers, where the conveyances were most often hand-carts and delivery wagons rather than carriages, past grim and dilapidated shops whose customers and keepers looked to be at the edge of desperation. We were accosted several times by beggars who, at a glance from one or the other of my escorts, faded quickly back into the shadows from which they had emerged.

I protested as we turned into a reeking alley.

"Keep moving if you value your life," I was told. The younger and scruffier of the pair added emphasis to the command, brandishing a pistol beneath my nose.

I looked for someone to call out to, but the few forms huddled against walls of the alley were candidates for the hospital, or more likely the morgue. Clearly, I was a captive and had little option but to obey or be brutalized. The brutality, as it turned out, was yet to come.

In short order I was pushed roughly through the door of a ramshackle tenement, shoved along a hallway and then manhandled down a flight of stairs into the darkness of a dank basement.

"Over there," came an order, directing me toward a bricked-in corner that, as

indicated by the black dust coating all surfaces, served as a coal cellar. At the moment it served as a small cell furnished with a shabby table and several old wooden chairs. I was guided, or rather, pushed, into one of the chairs.

"Shut up and sit still," the senior of the pair ordered as the other fastened a blindfold over my eyes. For what seemed hours, silence reigned. I heard nothing extraordinary, the room being much like a vault.

At some point another individual entered the room, and this an Englishman while my initial captors were, by their accents, Americans.

"Drink this," ordered the newcomer.

"I will not."

"We shall see about that."

There is little one can do once his jaw is forced open and his nose held shut. The liquid went down like fire and, despite the efforts of the two holding me, I coughed out about half of it.

"Again," ordered the newcomer, and the process was repeated.

"It is grain alcohol, often referred to as moonshine. Our American operatives, of course, make only the best. Although there are various alternatives, as you, a medical man, would undoubtedly know. We find that grain alcohol works quite well as a truth serum. Have another!"

"You will poison me!"

"Not yet."

I protested in vain. "If you are any sort of a gentleman you will forego this torture and explain your business. I have a serious allergy in regard to alcohol."

"How dreadful. Had I only known, I have might have brought nitrous oxide or some other substance." My tormenter's tone was sarcastic. "The fact is, Doctor, you and your cohort Holmes have relinquished the right to be treated as gentlemen in your determination to disrupt the activities of our organisation. We have scores to settle, particularly with Holmes, but you will do in the interim."

"Holmes is dead. I would have thought the word had spread among the criminal element."

"That sort of talk only provokes me, Doctor. Men, give him another dose. Perhaps we can induce a seizure."

"Why are you doing this?"

"We intend to get the truth out of you. Where is Sherlock Holmes?"

"Holmes is dead, I tell you. As any fool who reads the papers knows, he died at Reichenbach Falls, engaged in battle with Professor Moriarty, whom I suppose to be a former associate of yours."

By this point I was crashing in and out of consciousness, my senses muddled into a stormy ocean.

"Where is Sherlock Holmes?!"

"Dead. Dead. Dead, I tell you ... dead."

I was shaken violently from my stupor. "You had best answer! Where is Sherlock Holmes?"

The word wouldn't form. I could make only a stuttering "D" sound.

Even though almost blacked out, I do sometimes recall snatches of what has occurred. I believe I heard something like this:

"Watson, you befuddled fool, you have sealed your fate. Due to the blindfold you cannot see the chute above your head, but you will perhaps feel a sobering blast of air when it is opened. That it is opened indicates that the delivery truck has arrived with a load of coal. In the moments to follow you will either suffocate or be crushed. It is the least I can do to repay your meddling over the years. Goodbye, Doctor."

I faded from consciousness.

Sometime later, I awoke as the blindfold was pulled from my eyes. The light, though dim in that cellar, was blinding to me. As my eyes adjusted, I became aware of the presence of a uniformed officer.

"You are a lucky man, sir, very lucky."

"What's that? What is going on?"

"Had these fellows not questioned delivery to a site where no coal has been ordered for some years now, you would be another missing person. As it was, they thought their delivery instructions might have been in error and peered into the cellar. Now, who might you be, and what has happened here?"

I explained myself in accordance with the story you provided, that I was a British traveler on my way to the races at Saratoga.

"That may be," the officer responded. "Considering that you reek like a distillery, though, it appears you detoured to one of the dives nearby and were lured to your present situation by robbers taking advantage of your condition."

"The fact is, I was staying at a hostel catering to those who are abstaining from alcohol; I was abducted, subjected to torture, left to die by members of an international crime organization."

"Certainly you were, sir. Now, what I think is that you should curtail your drinking in low class bars. As a tourist, you are very much magnet for scoundrels."

In the interest of secrecy, I could not reveal that I was on a somewhat official mission. I sat in silence, struggling to collect my thoughts. There was nothing to be gained through argument with the officer. I envisioned a trip to his station and having to make my case to his superiors. To do so hardly seemed in my interests at that moment; fortunately it wasn't necessary.

The policeman put a hand on my shoulder. "This is New York City, sir. You can make a report if you wish, but there are a hundred robberies and more each day here, and there is little hope of resolution. Be more cautious of your companions in the future."

He helped me to my feet and after a few shuffling steps I found that I could keep my balance.

Watson further stated that he returned to the Volunteers shelter where, between prayer sessions, he was allowed to wash and was provided clean clothes. Upon my receipt of his letter, arrangements were made to supply him with funds to continue his journey.

Chapter Six

As he reported later, the doctor remained seated in the passenger coach for the first half hour of the journey, reading his newspaper. He then became restless and made his way to the lounge. As might be expected, the occupants were enjoying strong beverages and appeared to be in the best of spirits. So, like a moth to a flame, in short order he had consumed several whiskies.

To his credit, guilt found its way through the fog of drink and he was soon back to his seat and slumbering. In a tranquil state, he slept through his scheduled stop at Saratoga Springs. As a consequence, he was put off at the next stop, the popular resort community of Lake George. Getting back to Saratoga proved a bit of a problem, as can be seen from relevant passages of a letter preserved from that era.

In the interest of readability I will present his account in plain text and alert the reader upon its conclusion:

I left the train at Lake George, much concerned about having missed my stop, and made inquiries about traveling back down the line. The news was not good. I was told that due to a problem at one of the trestles, it might be some days before a train could pass in the direction of Saratoga Springs.

For the traveler with no mission in mind other than enjoyment of the scenery, my situation would not have presented any great dilemma. In my reading about the Lake George region I had come to know it as a first-rate tourist destination and summer home to many of wealth and fame. I was tempted to spend time exploring beside the uniquely clear waters of the Queen of American Lakes, over thirty miles in length, bordered by forests and adjacent to the regal Adirondack mountains. But my goal lay elsewhere.

You can imagine my consternation. I suppose it was obvious to anyone who observed me standing on the railway platform with valise in hand, staring this way and that in the hope a solution to my problem would present itself. In short order, a young copper-skinned lad with coal black hair was at my side, looking up.

"You need a ride somewhere, Mister?"

"I suppose I do. The train isn't running."

"Where to?"

"Saratoga Springs. Is there a coach?"

The little fellow frowned. "Folks travel by train, that's all there is. But come and talk to my father. He's going that way and wouldn't mind a passenger."

The father was a stocky fellow in bib overalls and a faded checked shirt, perhaps younger than his weathered features suggested. He stood beside an open wagon, watching as we approached with no particular show of interest but at the same time keeping us under observation.

"I am Dr John Watkins. The boy tells me you may be able to provide transportation to Saratoga Springs?"

"Jack Thibedeau, Doctor, and I'm just the man you're looking for, a guardian angel at your service in time of need. They say that trestle will be fixed in a few days but I know the boys sent to do the work and my bet is on a few weeks. Even then, it will be a risky business, crossing a trestle repaired by that crew."

I was to learn that this information was total fabrication; repairs were concluded satisfactorily over the next day. But I was the ignorant newcomer, and suffered the consequences. "Well, I don't care to wait. I have business down the line. But I must say that wagon of yours looks nearly ready for the woodpile. How far is Saratoga Springs?"

"Oh, it's just a short ways, sir, won't take no time at all, a gentle ride through lovely countryside. As for this sturdy, rugged vehicle and the trusty pair of steeds providing power, why, we've made it down from Canada in, what, son, seems just a couple of days? Record time."

"More like two weeks," the boy mumbled.

"Run along and fetch the others, that's a good boy, and we'll be on our way."

Others? My curiosity as to the meaning of the word in this particular situation was soon satisfied as two robust women and a small herd of youngsters appeared in the company of the lad who had lured me to the wagon.

"My wives and children," said Jack, smiling as he ushered and hoisted various of them into the already packed back of the wagon. "They like riding in the back, seeing where we've been."

The women commented but in a language unfamiliar to me. "You have two wives?"

"No, three. The other one is already down at the encampment, she walked down a few weeks ago to set things up."

"You say she walked?"

"Indians walk everywhere. An Indian has a horse, they get suspicious. My Mohawk grandfather has a horse, but he stays back in the mountains, doesn't bother with cities."

"But you have horses …"

"I'm half Indian, sure, but I'm Thibedeau. My father was French, my mother's Mohawk. I'm also a damn good cook when I want to be, a chef, and I know the big shots with mansions for summer homes. The constables give me trouble, I got folks to bail me out."

I learned quite a bit more about this fellow on our so-called gentle ride south, coursing a decent enough road that had its bone-rattling moments. Those moments were soon forgotten, though, as Thibedeau passed a jar of some homemade concoction.

"What is this beverage, if I may ask?"

"Applejack. Cure what ails you, right, Doc?"

I nodded rather than ask if we weren't by mistake drinking lantern fuel.

Thibedeau said he and his family were headed to an annual encampment just outside Saratoga Springs where they sold handicrafts and offered games of chance and other entertainments to the tourists.

Though rough at times the journey was not without its pleasures. We traveled under no ordinary sky; it was a vast canopy of brilliant blue, decorated with billowing clouds that seemed aglow with golden light. Thibedeau informed me that I was witnessing Adirondack weather at its best. "For every day like this one, there are dozens that are dark and gloomy."

Had I stuck to imbibing mountain air, my head would have been quite clear in no time. However, the jar passed back and forth, and forth and back. I do believe my brain went to sleep while I sat listening to Thibedeau. He entertained with wild tales, of having seen chariots of fire in the night sky and hairy creatures bigger than a man scampering through the forest and dragons poking their heads up out of mountain lakes.

Thibedeau's stories were amusing but I wanted to know about the area. I asked about his work. "I've been employed in rich folks' summer homes, as well as camps and hunting lodges, cooking for the big-shots. Last good job I had was chef for that actress, Langtry. Now that's a real woman, I tell you. But we had a little row. She didn't like the way I sliced the potatoes for frying, too thick."

"Odd sort of thing to have a row about."

"It got odder than that. I sliced those blessed potatoes so thin you could see through them."

"So you got fired, I take it."

"Not me, those thin-sliced potatoes were a tremendous hit with the guests. But I had obligations at our encampment, so I didn't stay on. I've been frying up those chips for visitors to the camp, though. They're quite popular."

He spoke over his shoulder and a bag was handed forward. "Try some," he offered. I did and I must say, he has come up with a tasty snack, a crisp potato wafer. However, this little delicacy is heavily salted and creates a thirst. A few more pulls from the applejack jar and I was nearly comatose.

Here concludes my selection from Dr Watson's letter. The tale, however, continues. As I have reconstructed it from subsequent conversations, I believe Watson's narrative would run about as follows:

Saratoga Springs is quite well known due its lofty position on the American horse racing circuit, and it is as well famous as a resort spa owing to the many mineral springs. Further, it is revered in America as a battlefield where British troops received a humiliating defeat. Actually, the town stands off some miles from the site of the battle.

The town is located in the foothills of the Adirondacks; the vast mountain range is not a looming presence as it is at Lake George, it is more a fanciful theme capitalized on by local merchants. There is a lake, cousin to the incredible assortment of lakes, rivers, streams and ponds of the adjacent mountain range. But compared to Lake George, Saratoga Lake is little more than a large puddle. It is large enough, though, to support an excursion steamboat and a number of private yachts, fishing boats and smaller recreational craft. While there is agitation in certain quarters to turn the Adirondack region into a public park, such a project would not extend so far south as Saratoga Springs.

To be honest, I had expected a crude and rustic frontier town masquerading as a resort. It had been my opinion that Americans were rough sorts like Davy Crockett and Daniel Boone, going about with their shirtsleeves rolled up, chopping down forests, building roads before knowing even where they would go.

I was quite surprised by the scene when Thibedeau shook me awake on an elegant elm-shaded avenue busy with coaches, buggies and bicycles. The avenue, wide enough for drilling a company of soldiers, led us to an aisle of truly colossal hotels, several taking up an entire city block each.

I was retrieving my valise when a policeman approached.

"You there! Get moving. no Indians allowed on the main street."

I protested. "Constable, this man was hired to convey me to my hotel, he is merely fulfilling his mission."

"You don't say? Then, I'll have you for consorting with Indians. You should keep better company."

Jack weighed in. "Constable, I am Thibedeau, the chef employed by many wealthy families of this city. Take care how you deal with us."

"And this mob in the back of your wagon, they're Pilgrims off the Mayflower no doubt? Move along, I tell you."

"This is a fine welcome to Saratoga Springs," I said to the officer.

My comment provoked the hard-eyed stare and folded arms of one whose tolerance is wearing thin. "Most of our visitors do not arrive in a way that attracts police attention, mister. I will be keeping an eye on you."

He stood by while I paid Jack. As the wagon pulled off, he gave me another cross look and strode away.

As it turned out, the first enormous structure that I noticed was merely a wing of the United States Hotel, a massive establishment with a quarter mile of colonnaded porches, and, as I later learned, a thousand rocking chairs lining its expanse of veranda. That awesome sight was rivaled by others, including the Grand Union, where, according to the instructions given upon my departure from England, I was to lodge.

The Grand Union is five stories of brick sprawled over a seven-acre site. Inside are corridors of two miles length in all. The bellhop, addressing my probable need for sustenance, announced proudly that the kitchen ordered 1,500 pounds of beef daily.

My rooms were opulent, quite beyond my needs or wants. I felt dwarfed and intimidated by the extravagant spaciousness and garish furnishings. I had both a front and back parlor, each arrayed with davenports and armchairs, and there was even a most annoying grandfather clock ticking away in a passageway. There were two enormous bedrooms decorated with frilly carvings and lace, a dining area with sideboard and chandelier, not to mention the expansive mirror-finished table which would comfortably seat a dozen.

Having examined the assortment of statuary and bric-a-brac and the fernery with its own fountain, I felt I had become resident of the showroom of an elegant home décor shop. I determined to find quarters more suited to my modest tastes as soon as possible, and it was not to be in one of the ostentatious hotels. Once settled, I would look into the problem of connecting with Mrs Langtry.

One table in my rooms was adorned with array of information for the tourist, and I was taken aback to find a Holmes Quarter on the map of the town. My inquiries revealed that this particular Holmes was a local undertaker, Ebenezer Holmes, who had built a block of town-homes as an investment.

Following a good night's rest and a robust breakfast, I set off through downtown at a brisk pace, crossing into an adjacent neighborhood of mansions, some imposingly ornate and others grotesquely gothic. I was to learn later that these are termed *cottages* by their wealthy owners who reside in them only during racing season.

Off along the side streets there were homes decidedly less pretentious, probably more typical of the residences likely to grace the main street of any prosperous American village. My guess was these were year-round, belonging to local well-to-do. Many of these domiciles, I was informed, are vacated by their owners during racing season, to be rented out at steep prices.

Arriving at a row of town-homes in the area shown on my map as the Holmes Quarter, I discovered a sign in one window offering rooms to let. This seemed a fortuitous solution to my interest in getting away from the hotel. I climbed the few steps to the front door and rang the bell. The lady who answered introduced herself as Mrs Hobson. Round-faced with gray hair, she was generally round, in a solid sort of way. Indeed, she had a second floor suite to let. I indicated my interest and offered to provide credentials.

Mrs Hobson shrugged at my offer. 'Payment is in advance,' she said. She showed me up a flight of interior stairs and into a sitting room. Whatever revival might come along in décor, Mrs Hobson was prepared. A delicate little ebonized desk was served by a massive gothic chair, while a pair of rattan chairs hemmed in a horsehair loveseat. Those furnishings offering display space were cluttered with an array of bric-a-brac and mementos from perhaps fifty years ago onward. Persons unknown peered out from two large oval gilt frames on a wall, while a host of other prints, from generic forest scenes to street scenes from foreign lands, vied with riotous floral wallpaper for attention.

"This would suit me quite well," I said.

On the way back down the stairs we encountered an elderly, nearly cadaverous gentleman with drooping white mustache. "Dr Watkins, Professor Varner," said Mrs Hobson. "The professor resides on the third floor. Dr Watson has taken the second floor."

"Delighted," I said, extending my hand. "In town for the races?"

He took my hand with reluctance and I felt as though I had, for a moment, taken hold of a warm slab of raw fish.

"Hardly. My area is Norse sagas," he said. "I am

translating them into French."

I should have given some thought to my reply but I said: "Why, ever?"

That prompted a truly disdainful look. "There is no story told in another language such as might not be improved by translation into French."

Chapter Seven

I continue my account of Dr Watson's adventure, mainly reconstructed as I recollect conversations. I believe I am providing a reasonably reliable narrative:

The hour was yet early in the evening but Watson, not yet having made his move to new quarters, had endured about all he could stand of the sounds of boisterous gaiety throughout the hotel, particularly the clinking of glasses and calls for more – more wine, more champagne, another round.

Thinking that a walk down the main boulevard might provide some relief, he set out. But the same sort of gay atmosphere prevailed, or so it seemed from sounds emanating from dimly lit clubs and cafes along Broadway. A drunk stumbled into his path and then proceeded to warn Watson to watch where he was going. He might have paid more attention to that warning, although ultimately the evening's events proved fruitful.

Nervous and despairing, battling temptation, Watson wandered into Congress Park. The park was shadowy, eerie, only slightly illuminated by dim and flickering gaslight, and that light only at its perimeters. It was a moonless evening. Towering trees stood guard and dense shrubbery crowded in on the isolated benches. A pond, where in the light of day children chased geese and lovers wandered as if in their own little worlds, now lurked as a dark and dangerous pit. Watson took a seat on a bench and tried to compose himself.

While attempting to ignore the sounds of music and happy voices coming from the nearby casino, Watson started at words spoken nearby. They were not so much words as growls. And suddenly he was confronted by three figures, men dressed more for millwork than for a night on the town in a resort spa.

"Crack off his fingers and feed them to the ducks. They'll eat anything."

"What is this? What do you want?" Even in the dark Watson could make out faces frozen in masks of metallic hardness. It was the pair who had lured him from the Salvation Army mission in New York City. That spoke for two of the men, while the third was unknown to him.

"It's your friend Sherlock we want, doctor. Where is he? And talk fast, mind you, or it's the worst for you."

"You're mad. I've told you, Sherlock Holmes is dead. Go away and leave me alone." Watson rounded the bench where he had been sitting, putting it between himself and his assailants. Turning abruptly, Watson dove into the bushes. But the thugs were on him in a moment and dragged him out like a hog about to be butchered.

"You're not worth the bullet, you quivering coward. We'll just frighten the life out of you." Two of his assailants held his arms while their companion put a pistol under his nose. "Where is he? Speak up!" The demand was followed by a brain-rattling cuff to the side of Watson's head. Watson felt faint but the toughs at either side held him up. "Let me go. You're talking sheer lunacy. Holmes is dead."

"One last time. Don't lie. Where is he?"

A commanding voice boomed from nearby. 'Here he is!"

The familiar voice was enough to assure Watson he had lost his mind, but a glance showed it was only the old professor from the rooming house, his spindly frame supported by a walking stick. "Flee! Run for your life," Watson warned. "Get the police."

The man with the pistol turned toward the interloper. "Don't interfere, you old coot. Get lost, and quick."

The professor's stick flashed like a whip and the pistol spun to the ground. Cursing, the thug grabbed at his elbow. Roaring in pain and anger, one arm hanging limp, he charged the professor with a remaining fist. "I'll smash you to a pulp!"

Again the stick flashed. This time at the man's knees, his legs buckled and he collapsed into a heap, hardly distinguishable from a pile of laundry. A crack to the head and his part in the fray was done.

One of Watson's holders let go and dove for the pistol.

A flick of the stick and the pistol was in the pond. Now Watson was released as both remaining assailants grabbed for the professor. He backed up, fists raised, smiling as they cursed.

Watson stood frozen in fear, knowing he should assist the elderly interloper but unable to move or even call out for help. Such was his affliction since taking to drink.

Incredibly, the professor's punches and jabs kept his opponents at bay. Then came the solid thud of fist on bone and one of the men was down. His partner pulled him to his feet. As the professor advanced to continue the fray, they ran off into the night.

"For goodness sake, Watson, sit down. There are enough statues in this park as is."

"Watkins is the name, as you may recall."

"Of course it is. Now, have a seat, you are looking pale."

Watson did as told and pulled in deep breaths in the hope of clearing his head. The elderly professor stood over the downed man, stick at the ready. Trying to shake off the effects of the stick, the thug looked around in disbelief.

"Your comrades have fled the field, it seems. Will you tell us who sent you or would you rather march along to the station house?"

Now it was Watson's turn to shake his head,

wondering if his senses had been distorted by a powerful blow. The words challenging the captive were in a voice all too familiar to him and yet that could not be.

"I've nothing to say," growled the thug. "Except that you'll get yours, Mr Sherlock Holmes."

"Not before you get yours, I'll wager. Your master does not abide failed missions."

As if suddenly aware of a fate worse than death, the grounded man spontaneously cringed and glanced side to side in search of an invisible enemy.

The professor flourished his stick. "Get out of my sight. Your cowardly countenance has told me all I need to know."

The man rose to a crouch then lurched to his feet and, cursing in the coarsest manner, stumbled off into the darkness.

"You must have knocked that fellow witless," Watson said as the professor joined him on the bench. "Did you hear him refer to you as Sherlock Holmes?"

Chapter Eight

"I imagine you are wondering, Watson, why I struck that fellow on the arm instead of directly on the hand that held the gun. Had I merely knocked the gun away, he would have been fit to scramble for it. As it was, his gun arm was totally disabled and it became a small matter to put him out of the action entirely."

"Yes, it was wonderful to see," said Watson. "But what I was wondering about, actually, is something which is very much awry here. You give every appearance of being Professor Varner, the upstairs lodger at my place of residence. But you sound like someone else."

Watson's comment evoked a tolerant smile. "I must confess, Watson, you have been victim of another of my little theatrical exercises. You should not be so surprised, having chronicled so many in your sensational accounts of my cases. I am not Varner, I am Sherlock Holmes."

"So the thug addressed you. But it is quite impossible. Holmes died at Reichenbach Falls."

"I am living proof to the contrary."

"And I am a medical man, so perhaps I can assist you in finding some help for your delusional condition. For one thing, you persist in calling me Watson when I have assured you that my name is Watkins."

The professor smiled again as might an adult when trying to explain sunrise to a child. "My condition is as I describe. I am very much Sherlock Holmes, and I am alive. I regret not having found a more delicate way of communicating to you the news that, for my own safety and for that of others, yourself included, news of my death was concocted."

Watson, believing that he was playing along with someone much disturbed, asked what threats the professor referred to.

"I refer to the remainder of Moriarty's gang. They would be watching, and any unusual activity on your part would put them on alert. A clear example, as I have heard from Mycroft, is your encounter in New York City. As soon as you made an unusual move, heading for the United States, they closed in."

Watson contemplated what he had heard for a few moments and then clenched his jaw decisively. He spoke like a schoolmaster tired of student pranks. "Your story is incredible. And yet, you do sound credible in the telling of it. Perhaps the name Varner is coincidentally similar to Vernet, a family Holmes descends from. It's all a bit much and, frankly, I find your amused stare most annoying. I do thank you for your assistance, whoever you may be, and I bid you goodnight."

The professor put a hand on his companion's shoulder and tightened his grip. Watson pulled away as if to acknowledge it was not the grip of a tired old man. "Hold on there, good old Watson. Come along for a bit of dinner and I shall tell my tale."

Watson sat scowling for a moment. "Name the basset hound that has been of assistance in several of your cases."

"Arnold."

"You see! You don't know, and you are a diabolical fraud!"

"The trouble is, you believe your tales and doubt the truth. His name was Arnold, but you found the name rather prosaic so you changed it to Toby," said the professor, rising to his feet.

"Oh. Yes. Quite right."

"Enough of this nonsense. I am far from recuperated from my recent adventures and this little exercise has quite worn me out. Let us find a restaurant and nourish ourselves, Watson."

On the main street, the professor led the way into a busy tavern. Watson surveyed the dim interior, seeing only a blur of shadowy shapes accompanied by a sound like swarming insects. "You know, I really don't think this is a place for me. I have developed an alcohol allergy, you see, and even the nearness of the stuff can have a bad effect."

"We shall have a booth and so will be out of sight

of the refreshments, Watson. We will send away the wine list, if any, and we will avoid sauces or any dish that might be, shall we say, contaminated. Do not forget that this is a spa known for its waters; it is very much in vogue to be *taking the cure*."

Over a decent American meal of steak, potatoes and salad, the professor pressed his claim. He said he was bruised and battered at the conclusion of the battle with his nemesis, the scholarly master criminal, James Moriarty. "I found myself in the role of the hunted as Moriarty's minions sought revenge. I could not stop to ask food or lodging, knowing my pursuers would use bribery, torture or any means fair or foul to learn of my whereabouts. I kept to the backcountry, living by my wits. My health deteriorated by the day, until at length I was discovered by the adventurer Sigerson as I lay nearly comatose in a remote Alpine shepherd's hut."

"With Sigerson's aid I was able to establish contact with my brother, Mycroft. I pledged Mycroft to secrecy and told him I must remain steadily on the move for a time to come. He was able to provide some resources but, still, there were the hardships of a fugitive life."

Watson cut in. "Mycroft is of course your brother, the connection is easily understood, but why did you not come to me for assistance?"

"Much as I might have wished to do so, I feared you would be under surveillance by my enemies. You are impulsive by nature and, if you will forgive me for the suggestion, might have taken some rash action believing it to be of benefit to me."

Watson's features fell in forlorn testimony to hurt feelings.

Sherlock reacted: "Dear Watson, my silence is a tribute to your bravery and courage, do you not see? You know very well you might have made some move which could have jeopardized us both."

Watson protested. "Your death, or my belief in it at any rate, cost me my courage. You saw me as those thugs attacked, frozen in fear, much like a statue, as you pointed out. Such has become a characteristic reaction."

"I had no idea your reaction would be so severe, and I deeply regret any wounds inflicted by my charade. I can only say it was a necessity. It will take some time to recover your strength and vitality, and your confidence. But soon it will be old times again, Watson. Let us cheer each other on."

"I wish I shared your optimism," Watson said, in a tone indicating serious doubt. "At any rate, you were going to tell me how it has been for you since last we met."

"Yes. Sigerson was all too pleased to join in the game. He would leave clues in various odd locales indicating the presence of Sherlock Holmes. Meanwhile, he recommended that I remove myself to Tibet for a time. I concurred with great enthusiasm, having several questions in mind about that culture that my visit might resolve."

"Even were my whereabouts to become known to my pursuers, I delighted in a vision of brutish louts from London's back alleys making their way through the perilous passes and treacherous gorges awaiting them in the Himalayas. Even greater was my delight in the thought that they might then pursue me back across Persia amongst wild tribesmen who screech savagely as they kick about the heads of their enemies like footballs. It was all quite interesting, learning the ancient secrets of warrior-monks in Tibet's remote monasteries, and then masquerading as an archeologist hunting pots as I made my way across the scrub-covered hills and desolate deserts of the Arab world. Still, my health had not recovered and my travels only taxed me further."

"At long last and near collapse I arrived in Monte Carlo. Having obtained a violin it was easy enough to pass myself off as a wandering gypsy entertainer. Until, that is, I encountered Mrs Lillie Langtry. As you will recall from the *Scandal in Bohemia* adventure in which you disguised her as Irene Adler, she has a knack for seeing through my impersonations."

"She keeps a villa there in Monaco, a lovely place surrounded by extraordinary gardens, with a grand view of the Mediterranean. It was a perfect setting for me to regain lost health out of sight of my enemies."

"It may surprise you that I committed myself to Mrs Langtry's care. It is true that, in the interest of preserving my energies for my work, I refrain from indulging in the sort of warm and intimate relationships that are the sanctuary or, as often, devil's den for the many. However, Mrs Langtry was most attentive and I was not entirely my usual self. We became quite close. Difficult to imagine, I suppose, but she is an extraordinary woman and has that power over men, at least in my experience."

Watson could hardly believe his ears. "Sherlock Holmes in love? It *is* difficult to imagine."

"Well, it was a short-lived affair, I assure you. What I felt will dwell in my heart for as long as it beats, Watson, but I could not abide her as a life companion. For all her attributes and graces, she is dizzily lost in a mental maze of her own design. The result is a stubbornness abiding no way but her own. I asked, for her own well-being, that she relinquish the amulet. She adamantly refused, and our relationship deteriorated from that point onward."

"You remain friends?"

"There have been exchanges of coded notes, but we haven't spoken since our parting in Monaco."

Watson's look was one of puzzlement. "But you have followed her here. Is that a protective measure?"

"Lillie Langtry is quite capable of taking care of herself. My interest is in recovering the amulet and, I should add, bringing down Moriarty's successor, Col

Sebastian Moran, when the time is right."

"You have tried again to obtain it from her?"

"Yes, and I believe the phrase 'over my dead body' was among the more cordial elements of her reply. That is why you have been called to action, Watson."

"It is a fool's errand. What is beyond your capabilities is certainly beyond mine."

Sherlock raised a warning finger. "Let us not presume, Watson. You possess qualities which have been integral to resolution of past cases and I am sure they abide with you now, if for the moment hidden in a self-created fog."

"I can only repeat, I wish I shared your optimism, Holmes."

Chapter Nine

Watson asked for further details about the nefarious Col Sebastian Moran. "I really do not know much about him," he said, "other than a bit from Mycroft. He certainly sounds a menace."

Sherlock thought for a moment and then said: "To those who know him casually, Col Moran is an austere, reserved gentleman, military in bearing, apparently of substantial means. Little would they suspect he is the heir to the vast crime network established by the late Professor Moriarty. In keeping with the tactic of his mentor, he does not flaunt his role publicly. To the extent he is known, it is as a daring sportsman, a stalker of man-eating tigers and rogue elephants, author of the rather popular book, *Three Months in the Jungle*. In certain circles he is also known as a no-limits gambler. Few other than myself are aware of his premier position in the Moriarty organization. As you may imagine, that privileged information adds to my being very much a marked man."

Watson told Holmes of British newspaper accounts indicating that authorities had smashed a major crime ring, which he assumed to be the apparatus left behind by Moriarty. "Do you mean to say it is revived?"

Holmes looked out into the room, as if to be assured there was no surveillance. "I have seen the pronouncement you mention. Moriarty, a braggart when not acting some part, told me once in the course of a gunpoint interview that I had no idea of the complexity of his web. And he was certainly correct at the time. As for the authorities, Watson, it is my observation that they are inclined to announce a minor success as the achievement of the end of crime as we know it. And the press and public are quite taken in, time and time again, by these pronouncements, which have become part of officialdom's stock in trade."

"So," suggested Watson, summarizing the briefing, "the network survived, and Moran is its new commander."

"The network is most assuredly recovering from damage done. I keep up with the situation thanks to packets of news clippings sent along by Mycroft. The signs of activity are there: a major jewelry theft that could only have been accomplished through strategies developed by Moriarty, or a gruesome murder that most certainly serves as a warning to rivals that the organization is conducting business as usual and will tolerate no competition."

"Of course, the structure is somewhat different under Moran. He is a dangerous and cunning sort but hardly the equal of Moriarty in cleverness and intelligence. Moran is man of the moment, a man of action, not a visionary schemer. My study of his character has proven a life-saving asset following the incident at Reichenbach Falls."

"How so?"

Holmes gazed at some remote vision occurring in his mind's eye. "To the mastermind Moriarty, there was perverse pleasure in waiting for the proper dramatic moment to take revenge. He might have attempted my extinction at other points in time but he chose the terrifying grandeur of remote Reichenbach Falls as a setting. Moran has no such flair. His thoughts are simply upon my assassination, playing hound to my hare, anxious to end the chase brutally and abruptly at the earliest opportunity."

Watson frowned. "Tonight's events would indicate he has seen through your latest disguise. By the way, Holmes, did you happen to notice the name of this establishment?"

"Yes, of course. It is a good old family name in this region. I am as safe here as in a bunker. Even Lestrade of Scotland Yard would pick up the clue were I to be ambushed in Moriarty's Pub."

At that point a metal object struck the back of the booth and clattered to the tabletop. The missile appeared to have been launched from the table of an obnoxious lot of rowdies who had been growling, cursing and hammering fists throughout the evening. Any one of the pack might have been responsible for a one-man crime wave, provided the crimes in question did not involve complicated thought or presentable appearance.

Holmes examined the object, a napkin ring. "I will just go and have a word with those troublemakers."

"Holmes, let us not get involved. There are four of them; regardless of their condition the odds are not in our favor. Having a word with that lot makes as much sense as having a word with a hornet nest."

At that point the manager, beads of sweat on his furrowed brow, appeared at their table. "My apologies, gentlemen, truly. That's a bunch from Captain Angus McSnay's boat, and I'll soon have to send for the constables."

Watson waved him off. "You've enough on your mind, my good man, don't be concerned about us."

Holmes was not so dismissive. "Someone should advise McSnay to discipline his crew."

"He'd laugh in your face, sir, at the very idea. They think it's clever to pitch things at the staff to get their attention. It's not as though they've singled you out for that treatment; they just missed their target, a waiter. I shouldn't have let them in. At any rate, your meals are on the house tonight, and again, my apologies."

The manager strode to the source of the disturbance. Rather than quieting the crew, his intervention only inspired more boisterousness and belligerence. "Those pretty dandies complaining about us? We'll show 'em good manners!"

At that, another missile flew in the direction of Holmes and Watson. This time Holmes plucked it from the air as though picking fruit. He rose from his seat. "We should be going, I suppose."

"I know you would prefer to settle with them, Holmes, but I am just not up for it. My stomach is churning."

Watson stood to join his companion. A call came from the far table. "Don't run off, Nancy, the night's still young!" The outburst was followed by hoots and guffaws.

Holmes hefted the latest of the napkin rings that had flown across the room. "I really should return this," he said, pitching it in an arc so that it landed precisely as he intended, with a splash in a pitcher of beer at the far table.

The effect was a chorus of rage. The offended rogues rose up, each as if dancing to a tune different from one heard by the others, knocking over chairs and scattering glassware. With belligerent curses, taunts and threats, they made a stumbling charge toward Holmes and Watson, who were swiftly through the door.

"This way!" Holmes turned from the main avenue to a shadowy, refuse-strewn alleyway.

Watson glanced over his shoulder as he made the turn and saw that the motley crew was still in pursuit. "I am not as quick as you, Holmes, we must find a policeman to put a stop to this."

"And how will I explain my disguise? 'Yes, officer, I am in fact Sherlock Holmes, recently returned from the dead.' Is that it, Watson?"

Watson's run was something of a hop, given his old leg wound. "I would fare no better, masquerading under the name of Watkins."

They made their way through the alley and out to another side street. "We'll duck in here." Holmes took Watson by the arm and steered him into a shop. Watson glanced at the sign above the door: Literate Mallard Bookshop.

He surveyed the wall-to-wall books. "Saints preserve us. You might at least have chosen a gun shop, Holmes."

"Any port in a storm, Watson."

The shopkeeper, cozy as a cat in an armchair behind a glass display case and counter, looked up from the book he was reading. "Hello, Johnny," said Holmes. "Thugs – and a few too many for us to handle."

"Welcome, Professor. How interesting. Well, I have no other company at present, follow me." The shopkeeper tripped the lock on the front door and led the callers along an aisle of books toward another room.

"Wait here while I see what's going on," the shopkeeper advised. In moments he returned. "Quite an ugly bunch. Looks like some of the pirate crew from *Treasure Island*. They've gone on down Phila Street, most likely they'll stumble into the next pub they come to."

Holmes expressed his gratitude with Watson providing an echo. The shopkeeper shrugged. "You don't get a lot of excitement in a bookshop; the diversion was welcome. But you'd better stay until we're sure they have cleared out. What prompted the attack?"

"They were behaving badly up at Moriarty's Pub," Sherlock explained. "We became objects of their buffoonery. There was a bit of a confrontation; my friend did the maths and suggested a hasty retreat."

Watson meanwhile had wandered into another room where local crafts were on display.

"Ah, yes, your friend. We haven't been introduced."

Holmes, known to the proprietor as Professor Varner, led the way into the room where Watson was examining rustic baskets. "Dr Watkins, may I present Johnny Sophie, our benefactor and owner of this marvelous literary labyrinth. Dr Watkins is visiting from London."

Cordialities exchanged, Watson asked if the crafts were local.

"I get them from a secretive group that lives remotely in the mountains, they say the only way to their hideaway is to follow what's called The Forgotten Trail. It's got that name because no one can tell you how to find it. They've a castle beside Lake Gaggamaggatt, a lonely, isolated place where no one in their right mind would be caught dead. The castle, they say, is a remarkable structure, built years ago out of logs hewn square, with huge stone turrets, towers and chimneys. It's a fellow named Trogg brings these things into town, he's said to be the leader of the group. He goes by the title of Reverend, though I do wonder how he came by it."

"So it is a religious colony, is it?" Watson asked.

"Don't know as that's what you'd call it. You hear only rumors but it's said to be an odd, rough-looking lot hangs out up there, most likely deserters and drifters, escapees and outcasts, outlaws and renegades. One fellow who'd seen the place said the occupants were the sort who had no hope of Heaven and no fear of Hell. Trogg keeps them busy at handicrafts. As you see, twig brooms, sap pails, scoops, dippers …"

Watson's gaze followed the sweep of Sophie's arm to survey the collection. "It seems a good thing someone's keeping up the traditional crafts, what with the trend being toward factories and mass production these days," the doctor remarked.

"To be honest, look closely and you'll see this is fairly shabby craftsmanship. When I was growing up we made everything from cradles to coffins by hand. We used good strong wood, oak, fruit or nut wood, not this old soft pine. And, look closely, there's no detail to the work."

Holmes examined a slotted spoon. "I see what you mean. It's so rough-hewn, one could get a splinter. And you have suspicions about this fellow Trogg?"

"He claims to be a man of the cloth and all the while has a bizarre obsession with Lillie Langtry; you know who I mean, the actress? She has a mansion and stables near here. Trogg, he's always asking for the latest magazines where he might find pictures accompanying Lillie Cream, Lillie Powder and Lillie Bustles, as well as reproductions of paintings by Whistler and several others."

"He is hardly alone in that regard," Holmes said. "The men line up the night before to get good seats for her shows. She puts a particular feather in her hat and the fashion trade wipes out an entire species of birds to meet the demand for more of the same."

"True, true. The other odd thing about Trogg is his fascination with anthropodermic bibliopegy."

Watson raised a questioning eyebrow. "How's that again?"

"Not the sort of thing he'd find here in this shop, but he never fails to ask. It refers to books bound in human skin."

"Can't say as I care for the sound of that," Holmes said. "After all, the quality most commented upon regarding Lillie Langtry is …"

"Of course," said the bookman, "the beauty of her skin."

Chapter Ten

I will continue my tale with my own recollections as supplemented by conversations and letters.

Correspondence between Sherlock, Watson and myself was a two-way affair, and I apparently erred in passing along to Watson news that I thought would be of great relief to both men concerning the whereabouts of Col Moran.

Watson received my letter during the strange days following the incident at Moriarty's Pub, during which, to Watson's distress, he observed Holmes slipping out at all hours in various guises; now an unshaven workman with a lunch pail, next a regal coachman.

Watson employed himself in walks about town, taking in the track and the world's finest collection of thoroughbreds strutting and prancing through their exercise workouts, visiting the shady parks and their renowned springs, strolling the side-streets to observe the latest architectural innovations as one tycoon vied with the other for the most ostentatious dwelling. Upon his return he would often note Holmes peering from a window at a crouch, flitting from one vantage point to another. Once he saw him entering the house by the coal cellar.

Curiosity and concern getting the best of him, Watson called at his friend's door. "What is going on, Holmes? This behavior is most peculiar, even for you."

"Detecting, Watson. That is what I do, haven't you noticed? I want to determine whether Moran has us under surveillance."

"But Mycroft has assured me in his latest that Moran is nowhere near Saratoga Springs. According to Mycroft, the villain is pursuing rumors that you are to be found in the wilds of the Middle East. Your brother has had reports from his agents."

Holmes waved off Watson's comment. "His agents indeed. Opium-besotted brigands who wouldn't know Moran from Queen Victoria; that is whose word my brother is taking. Is it at all conceivable that they might fabricate sightings in order to keep the gold coin flowing in their direction?"

"It is possible."

"Quite so."

"If Moran were hereabouts and aware of your presence, why would he not attempt to assassinate you?"

With a frown of impatience, Sherlock explained: "He may be impulsive but he values his skin, Watson. This is not the wild western part of the country where shots may be fired and no questions asked. Not only are the town constables on alert for mischief, the place is also thick with private security personnel hired by the track and its wealthy patrons."

"So he must remain concealed, I take it, and strike from ambush?"

"We can assume he is operating in disguise. In tourist season, nearly everyone in town is a stranger. We cannot tug at every beard or pull at every mustache. What do we know of this Captain McSnay, or of the mysterious Trogg, up in the mountains? As for assassination, I have not given him opportunity for ambush. Were we in London, he would be on familiar ground and escape might be easily accomplished. Here, he does not know the shortcuts, alleyways, secret passages or other routes that would serve the criminal in avoiding public notice."

"But no doubt he will strike at the first opportunity."

"An opportunity he must create, Watson. I am going on the hypothesis that he is looking for bait that will lure me into a deadly trap."

Following that discussion, Holmes retreated to his room, refusing to answer when Watson came to call, or, if he did come to the door at all, speaking hardly a word from behind a thick veil of pipe smoke, apparently in the throes of melancholy and lethargy. Watson feared he had taken up cocaine again.

Mrs Hobson brought up trays of cold cuts, cheeses and breads that remained outside Sherlock's door. When Watson threatened to break down that door, he answered and insisted he was merely fasting, an amusement he had come to appreciate when inducted into a mystic order in Persia. "I find the hallucinations brought on by fasting to be most interesting."

Watson was having none of it. "This problem is medical, not mystical. You have all the symptoms of a serious mental disturbance. It may be due to nicotine poisoning, as you have turned the room blue with smoke. If you will not listen to me, I will call in a local physician."

With a faraway look in his eye, Holmes offered a thin smile. "You have deduced that I am a victim of some sort of brain fever, mad, or getting there, why bother with a second opinion? Have the courage of your convictions, man. What do you propose? To sedate me, shoot me full of morphine perhaps? I can manage that without your assistance, thank you."

"It is not my intention to insult or anger you, Holmes. Certainly you are no more mad than I, if that is any consolation. But your behavior perplexes me."

"I appreciate what I take to be a vote of confidence, Watson. Call it boredom. The opportunity has not yet presented itself for you to attempt retrieval of the amulet, there is really nothing for us to do until such time."

"And you suppose you are alone in your state of mind? I am also growing weary of doing nothing."

Sherlock waved to indicate the way down the hall. "Well, then, by all means, take yourself off to the grand hotels and attend the hops, as do most other revelers in this gay resort. Be off with you. Have a good time."

Watson drew himself up in indignation. "You know very well I do not participate in events where alcohol flows, and I have never been one for entertainments such as you suggest."

"Calm yourself, I am but goading you to find your own amusements, my dear friend. Be assured, I will advise you the moment we have work to be done." With that, Holmes withdrew again to his sanctum.

What had initially been the walking tours of a sightseer for Watson became purposeless roaming, aimless wandering up one street and down the other. It was upon his return from one of these rambles that he found a note pinned to his door. Opening the note, he discovered a message from Sherlock requesting that they meet the following morning at a nearby intersection, and that he await the detective's arrival if he was not present at the specified time.

"It seemed a ridiculous request," Watson recalled. "Surely he could more easily call for me at our rooms. I could only assume he had reasons beyond my immediate understanding."

A clue to those reasons lay in the concluding sentence of the note, "Perhaps in keeping this appointment you will find a respite from your boredom."

The next morning following breakfast, Watson marched off in the direction of the meeting site. "I dared not speculate as to the purpose of the meeting," he told me long afterward. "There had been altogether too many occasions upon which I had accepted praise from Holmes for my conclusions, only to have him set those conclusions on their heads in his final comment, usually remarking that I had missed the point almost entirely but that my fallacious assumptions had helped guide him to the truth of the matter."

"Though certain I had followed Holmes' instructions to the letter," Watson continued, "he was not to be found at the designated corner. I waited patiently for a time and sallied four blocks this way and four blocks that, and over again, encountering no one save an elderly gardener tending an overgrown flower bed. Had Holmes met with some harm? At last, in frustration, I inquired of the old man who was grimly attacking a host of intruding weeds whether he had perhaps seen someone of my friend's description."

As I recollect from Watson's account, the tale continued:

The old man assured him that, yes, he had indeed seen such a fellow, and pointed a trembling finger toward the rear of the house behind him. "But dadburn it," said the fellow, "he seems to have disappeared. Wait here and I'll take a gander." As if there was great effort involved in putting one foot ahead of the other, he tottered toward the back of the residence and turned behind it. And, shortly, Sherlock in his Professor Varner disguise emerged.

"What game is this?" Watson demanded.

Holmes carried a rental sign which he plunged into the front lawn. "There," he said, "I might as well leave it as I found it."

"That was you, then, the old gardener?" Watson fumed. "You are having a joke at my expense."

"It is no joke, my dear Watson. I had to assure myself that you were not being followed by our enemies. While they may have high regard for my ability to detect a stalker, the same may not be true in your case."

Watson's temperature was rising. "And has this silly exercise been to some avail? I have applied a keen eye to my surroundings since my arrival here, on the lookout for you, though I would have noticed anyone else. So, are you assured that I am not under surveillance?"

"To the contrary, I am certain you are accompanied by at least three clandestine escorts."

Watson glanced about in all directions, mystified by the observation. "I have seen none."

Holmes smiled indulgently. "No, but you have played your part incredibly well, Watson. I imagine our watchers have been driven quite to the edge of their wits, very possibly stumbling over each other as they scrambled to keep up with your peripatetic meanderings."

Watson was fast approaching a fit of temper. "So I am now relegated to the status of decoy. A fine thing. I am a mere wooden duck floating on the pond of your plots and schemes."

"My apologies," said Holmes. "But of course you must see that you are the hero of this episode. It is your performance that has exposed those shadowing you. Bravo, Watson, well done."

Watson accepted the praise with some reservation. "Should I ever again find myself in such a situation," he declared, "I shall tear the grey hair off the nearest bystander to expose another of your games."

"Let us hope your assumptions are accurate in such a case," said Holmes. "Come along, now, let us give your unseen friends a bit of exercise."

The pair set off at a brisk pace in the direction of the elite residential section noted for enormous, show-place homes. As they conducted their prowl, Holmes embarked on a lecture regarding his thoughts on the architecture of their host country. Watson attempted to listen carefully as his companion delineated the various influences that had shaped an eccentric departure from the staid structures –- such as colonial and federal –- that were typical of earlier periods in America. As they walked down Lake Street, Holmes pointed out various novelties of modern residential design.

"There, you see that? A ridge turret, a little observation station jutting up from the roofline."

"I might call such a thing a belfry."

"You might," Sherlock conceded, "and others would possibly use the terms belvedere or cupola. My point is not so much to achieve absolute precision in labeling these ornaments. I am not an architect, Watson. But I do have good reason for making these observations, I assure you."

If so, Holmes seemed in no great rush to share those reasons with Watson, who was much on the alert for any clue. Watson recalled: "I would say the better part of an hour went by, and I must admit I grew somewhat weary of standing in front of this or that great pile of wood, brick or stucco while Holmes carried on about parapets, high-pitched gables, dormers, chimney pots and balconies."

There came a point where Watson expressed his frustration. "You know, Holmes, we are wasting a great deal of time parading around like tourists while getting no nearer the amulet. Is there not some more productive way we might spend our time, or, if not, would it be of great inconvenience if we continued this effort another time and set about finding ourselves a decent meal? I am near starvation."

Holmes turned a deaf ear to the plea and prattled on about portals, towers, bays, porches and widow's walks. Watson had thought their path would lead down Lake Street toward the center of town, but then, much to his disappointment, Holmes veered onto Circular Street at the rear of Congress Springs. After a few blocks they stood in front of Ambassador Batcheller's rarely occupied home, an eccentrically monumental structure inspired to some degree by Mad Ludwig's castle in the Bavarian Alps.

Holmes pointed out influences ranging from German gothic to Islamic. Owing to the small lot, a pedestrian might view the mansion from many perspectives, and this seemed his intention. With Holmes in the lead, they walked round and round, started off in one direction and turned back abruptly, then stepped across the way to a little park surrounding a springs and moved about to inspect the mansion from yet other angles.

Watson's patience had reached its limit. "I can endure this no further. I am accompanying you at your invitation on this senseless foray, but I must say it appalls me that you are so willing to waste precious time. I for one feel compelled to be of what service I can in the case at hand. I must bid you good day."

Holmes' arched eyebrows conveyed to Watson the feeling of being a bug under observation by a very detached entomologist. "Do you wonder at all how it is that I have made such a study of the architectural novelties such as have been pointed out to you, Watson?"

"I suppose there must be some purpose," the doctor confessed grudgingly. "You are a walking textbook on the subject."

"It is simply a matter of self preservation. Saratoga Springs is a dream location for the ambusher and assassin. In structures of the colonial or federal periods in this country, the person of murderous intent may choose a rooftop or window as a vantage point, and that is about the sum of the options. But the vogue in this city, featuring designs of the great fortresses, castles and cathedrals, all wrapped in pure gothic fantasy, offers a multitude of murderous possibilities."

"All right, I accept that it is in my interest to be more observant. But what is the particular application to our current situation?"

"Had you paid closer attention, Watson, you might have noticed that thug spying on us from the parapet of a mansion half way up Lake Street. No doubt one of Moran's hirelings. Or as we turned the corner, a fellow whom I take to be an American private investigator lurking behind the spindles of a high porch, no doubt a Pinkerton man. And need I mention a member of the local constabulary I noticed ducking from view in the minaret tower atop Ambassador Batcheller's mansion? And I may not have noticed all; we must also take into account Mycroft's spies, who may have been more successful at concealment. I would say the lot of them are probably quite fed up with the hide and seek game we have been playing as we made our rounds this afternoon."

Watson, in his dismay looking like some large wilted plant, stood in silence staring morosely at the pavement.

He later offered this observation: "Mine was a cruel fate, always to be outdone by the great detective. But I shook myself back into a better frame of mind. With jaw set, I reminded myself of my role as chronicler. There was some comfort to be found in viewing myself as the lantern, casting a light on Sherlock's remarkable feats for public view. Were matters left to his own doing, his talents would be known only to readers of a few obscure scholarly journals."

At a signal from Sherlock, Watson looked up to see the constable who had earlier harassed Thibedeau and himself, attempting unsuccessfully to flatten against a wall of the tower atop the Batcheller mansion. It appeared that a barrage of uncomplimentary remarks was passing the officer's lips.

"Whatever can they hope to gain by following us around town, Holmes?"

"No doubt their hopes vary. The thug is probably assigned to alert his superiors regarding our movements. The detective may hope we will lead him to outlaws sought by the Pinkerton Agency. The local constable seems to view you as a prospective source of mischief and feels compelled to keep you under close watch. As for Mycroft's minions, they are simply acting as his eyes and ears."

Watson pondered this analysis. "I see. And now, shall we make a dash and give them the slip?"

"Oh, I think not, Watson. Such an effort might put some excitement into their tedious tasks. Let us dawdle and take a leisurely stroll along this path and that alleyway to see if we cannot bore them to distraction."

"I won't. Enough is enough. You go on with your cat and mouse, Holmes. If any choose to follow me, they may endure the torment of watching while I dispatch a hearty meal. Given that they have been following us all this time, quite possibly they are as hungry as I am."

"Ah yes, food. You mentioned it hours ago, didn't you? A secondary matter to me at times such as this."

"You are some sort of automaton, a machine with no appetite. But surely you are not criticizing my wishing to nourish myself? Your ascetic ways are not for the normal person."

Holmes' smirk betrayed a fondness for being described as out of the ordinary. "As you wish, Watson. Being so concerned about the amulet, it surprises me that you would devote energy to digestion that could be applied to more serious matters."

"As it happens, Holmes, I view sustenance as a serious matter. I have had enough of playing the worm on your hook, cheese for your rats, feed for your chickens. I leave you to your fox and hounds amusements."

"I shall continue to entertain the menagerie to the best of my ability, and good afternoon to you then."

Watson strode off in the direction of town.

A replenishing meal did little to improve Watson's mood. In hopes of finding some solace by the water's edge, he hiked to Lake Saratoga. His thoughts, he told me later, took a dark turn. "I began to wonder if Holmes' critique of my behavior might be deserved. I was overtaken by a feeling of guilt, my conscience suggesting that I should have stayed and assisted as he engaged our pursuers. Upon reflection, it was not the grandest mistake I had ever made -- but in my melancholy I had built the mole hill into a mountain."

He was walking by the lakeside in the late afternoon, brooding, and it happens that by the lakeside there were two types of commercial establishments, one being the bait shop serving fishermen and the other the tavern serving alcohol. Saratoga Springs went through wet and dry spells, depending upon which influences weighed heaviest in the ballot box. At this particular time, the imbibers ruled.

Watson passed by several of the taverns but at last turned in to one, his idea being to follow the American tradition of a coffee after his meal. "As you know, it is the considered in our country to be the beverage of bohemians and temperance crusaders," he told me later. "I had tried a cup and felt I was tasting watered down soot. But the thought that I was merely following custom was sufficient to trick my mind."

Once inside, of course, he decided against coffee, instead concluding that one small beer would have no effect on him other than that of refreshment.

As might be expected, one small beer led to one large beer and, as day evolved into early evening, Watson continued his binge to a point where he was, as they say, three sheets to the wind. He vaguely recalled switching from beer to whiskey but had no distinct recollection. And the upshot of it was that he was arrested for murder.

Chapter Eleven

We have only the report of the local police as to what occurred that evening, Watson being an unreliable witness due to his inebriated state. It happened that a constable was patrolling, walking by the darkened lakeside docks, as it was not unusual at a late hour to encounter the disoriented tourist in need of assistance. At first the constable thought he had found just such a person in the drunken Watson, stumbling about and muttering incoherently. Then he noticed nearby the prone figure later identified as that of Lillie Langtry's chef, name of Pettigrew, who, upon closer examination, was found to be mortally wounded. Due to his proximity and condition, Watson was immediately suspect. The constable eagerly set upon him and put him in handcuffs.

Watson was taken to the police station and charged with the crime of murdering Pettigrew. He was taken for a very suspicious character, as he had to explain that he was Dr Watson traveling as Dr Watkins. The façade did not sit well with the authorities; they took it as an indication that they had in hand a nefarious criminal. The outcome of it all was that word reached Sherlock of Watson's situation, presenting him with something of a dilemma.

Sherlock, of course, had gone to some pains to avoid the public eye, and this was surely a case that would promptly become a sensation. To go immediately to Watson's aid and reveal his true identity, as he must when presenting himself to the local authorities, promised to provoke more problems than it might solve.

For one thing, the glare of publicity would make it difficult for him to be of clandestine assistance in investigation of the charges against his friend. Further, revealing his true personnae would expose him to the attention of Moran and his thugs, a problem he did not wish to contend with while attempting to be of help to Watson.

Sherlock decided that under these circumstances his best course of action would be to ask Lillie Langtry to intervene. Given her connections, he believed she might accomplish a great deal, while efforts on his part would only further complicate the matter. Mrs Hobson not being on the new telephone line, and being distrustful of the device under any circumstances, Sherlock dispatched a note to Mrs Langtry. In the note he said that surely she would not consider Watson a likely suspect and would assist in obtaining his freedom.

Mrs Langtry replied that she would contact her friend, a local judge. As it turned out, even in so serious a case as a murder charge, bond could be arranged at the judge's discretion. Mrs Langtry posted bond and Watson was soon a free man, pending a forthcoming hearing. He was warned to remain in the vicinity.

In her reply to Holmes, Mrs Langtry mentioned that some of her jewelry was missing, and she expressed the hope that Sherlock would look into the matter. "Of course, such a concern is secondary to your efforts on behalf of Dr Watson. However, I know you have sought the amulet given to me by a special someone. It is among the missing pieces.

"Should you find the amulet, I trust you will return it to me. It is mine by right, given as a gift. If the giver desires its return, he should have the courage to ask in person. Of course, there is the possibility that you are the engineer of this theft; however, I am much more inclined to suspect the late Pettigrew."

"Also troubling," she continued, "at a time when I must devote my attention to replacing the deceased chef, is the apparent disappearance of William Yates, the butler. Chefs are plentiful in this town but a good butler is hard to find."

Watson, recovering his senses but yet in a state of shock, was beginning to realize more fully the implications of recent events. "I shall jump from a bridge, Holmes. Mary will never take me back once she hears of this. And I do not even know whether I am guilty or not."

Sherlock's reaction to Watson's despair was casual. He shrugged. "Look on the bright side, Watson, you have given us something to apply ourselves to – a mission."

Watson was far from mollified. "There is no bright side. My situation is hopeless. I must have done it; they even have a witness against me."

"Ah yes, the witness. An old Indian known only as Joe who prowls the town begging for coins to support his thirst for whiskey. At one time he was a respected leader in the Bear Clan, but he has fallen into a desperate way of life. I know his reputation; it is that he will attest to whatever is wanted in exchange for a jug. It is a pity but that is what the white mans' firewater has wrought among those people."

"You are saying the constabulary bribed him?"

"Not necessarily, it may have been the perpetrator. I tracked him down but could obtain nothing more than babbled incoherencies."

"Then he can be shown to be unreliable. Still, I cannot prove my innocence."

"We must find another explanation for the murder."

"What other explanation can there be?"

"At the moment I cannot say, Watson. I have examined the site of this debacle but find myself short on useful data at present."

Watson asked if Holmes had an idea regarding whom Pettigrew might have met at lakeside.

"Subjects unknown. There was far too much coming and going of authorities and curiosity seekers. But from tracks left prior to the arrival of the crowd, someone sped off to the west in a cart. Who and why, I do not know, but there is likely a connection to Pettigrew's death."

"It gives me hope. But you have no other clue?"

"Just this." Holmes held out a hand displaying a small golden bead.

"And what is that?"

"A bit of jewelry. I found it in a rut near the scene. It must have been spilled by whoever fled in a wagon."

"What significance could that have?"

"I've reached no conclusion. A line of thought is that if there is one golden bead, there were many. If there were many, there was jewelry. If there was jewelry, perhaps there was an amulet."

Watson brightened a shade. "And perhaps Pettigrew stole the jewelry, including the amulet. Yates, the butler, pursued him. They fought and Pettigrew was killed."

"Brilliant deduction. And where is Yates now? Why didn't he return the jewelry?"

"He had killed Pettigrew. He fled the area with the jewelry and left me to face charges."

"So my observation is incorrect –- there was no third party at the scene. In a wagon, for instance?"

"I don't know, Holmes. It is hopeless. I feel the

gallows rope tightening around my neck."

"Then I should reconsider my involvement in this investigation."

Watson could not believe his ears. "Whatever can you mean by that?"

"I mean that my methods will invariably lead to the truth of a matter, Watson. What would be our course of action should I discover that you are indeed the culprit? Suppose you interrupted some sort of nefarious activity, an exchange involving stolen goods, and were set upon by Pettigrew? Suppose you acted in self-defense but, owing to your state of inebriation, cannot even testify as to the circumstances?"

Watson raised his arms in a gesture of helplessness. "Shameful, isn't it? Except that in my state of mind, it would be more likely that if Pettigrew had set upon me, the body at the shoreline would have been my own. I have not been exhibiting great courage of late."

"I am inclined to agree. My threat to withdraw was issued in hopes of shocking you out of self-pity," Sherlock declared. "You know that I prefer those clients who protest their innocence in the face of great odds to the contrary."

"And so, I am now reduced to status of client?"

"For goodness sake, Watson, shake loose of this dejection. Of course you are more than a client, and together we have faced situations more daunting than this one. Snap out of it, man."

"I am only accepting that I have brought this catastrophe upon my own head, Holmes. That is not the sort of observation that brings cheer."

Holmes said it might do both of them good to take in Mrs Langtry's performance at the Opera House. "It will help clear the clutter from our minds if we focus for a bit on lighter matters."

Watson argued that he was in no mood for entertainment, but, at Sherlock's insistence, agreed to attend.

Chapter Twelve

What I know of Lillie Langtry is only what I have read in the newspapers and the odd bits of intelligence – I cannot bring myself to call it *gossip* though of course it was – surrounding her affair with Prince Albert Edward, a matter which occasionally required my intervention.

According to the papers, when she first appeared in New York she was mobbed by hysterical fans. She could not go out on the street and had to travel incognito. Her rooms were so full of flowers, candy, fan mail and every conceivable sort of gift up to and including two pianos, it was nearly impossible to move about within. Tickets to her first performance were in such demand that the theater auctioned them to the highest bidders rather than sell them outright.

Relying on memory of conversations over the years, I will reconstruct events of the evening's performance (or, as it turned out, non-performance) as best I can. Watson, his spirits somewhat lifted, said he was looking forward to the programme, having read that Mrs Langtry had surprised critics with her command of Shakespeare.

Sherlock was not so surprised. "She is quite

talented, Watson, and a serious student in areas of interest to her. Those drawn by her beauty are often taken aback to find she also possesses quite a good mind."

Upon surveying the crowd gathered for the evening's performance, Watson concluded that, in terms of ostentation, the American rich were by far superior to the elite of London. If he thought he had seen finery in observing the promenades down Saratoga's main avenue, Broadway, those were casual affairs in comparison to the shine of silk and the flash of jewelry on display at the theatre. There were grand entrances as certain patrons arrived in coaches drawn by the proudest of horses, attended by coachmen, footmen, even buglers.

Despite the warmth of the evening, the ladies were turned out in a dazzling array of jewel-studded capes, plush opera coats and shimmering wraps. A good gust of wind, should one have passed through, would have gathered up a serious fortune in the most fashionable hats and bonnets.

"Watch your pocket. If there are not a dozen handsomely bedecked thieves working this crowd, I would be most amazed," Holmes muttered. Watson made no reply, mesmerized by the sparkle of precious stones decorating both ladies and gentlemen. Here a brilliant necklace the size of a horse-collar, everywhere stickpins sporting cut gems fit for a royal crown, or pearls as large as marbles, and three glittering rings to a hand was a common sight.

"It is easily seen why the jeweler Tiffany has a local branch," Watson said at last.

Watson wished he had paid more attention to the photo-engravings and sketches in American newspapers, feeling certain they must be in the midst of any number of celebrities. Holmes was not in the least intrigued, making his way through the crowd of gaudy peacocks as if through a pen of cattle.

Within the hall, Watson remained in awe. "This is among the most marvelous rooms I have ever seen," he declared. "The glitter of patrons aside, why, the chandeliers put Earth's celestial dome to shame."

"Poetic, Watson. I envisage the time coming when the entire world will be aglow from one day to the next, when darkness will disappear altogether and stars will be invisible. Personally I much prefer the night sky over Sussex Downs to this garish and conspicuous exhibition."

It was just as well that Watson found fascination in the glamour of the audience and the grandness of the hall and its décor, for they were not to see Lillie Langtry that evening. Curtain time came and went. When there was still no sign of the entertainer after the passage of a quarter of an hour, the occasional murmurings of the audience became a low hum of conversation.

Holmes sat meditatively, eyes closed.

Watson scanned the aisles, the doorways at either

side of the stage, the stage itself, and then the same again. "What can be the matter?"

"It is not uncharacteristic," Holmes replied. "You know how I feel about punctuality; I think it is the worst of manners to keep another waiting without serious justification. In Lillie's case, I could either accept tardiness or forget our engagements altogether. She is truly, as the jest goes, one who could be late to her own funeral."

"I sense something of a resentment."

"I won't deny it. I do not enjoy being ushered in after everyone else is seated, or making excuses to my hostess, or, often as not, missing an event altogether because of someone else's unmannerly habits."

"Are you not concerned that some difficulty may have befallen her?"

"What is the likelihood that she could not send word? Here is the manager again, so we shall see."

At the half hour, the theatre manager appeared from behind the curtains. "Ladies and gentlemen. My deepest apologies. Due to circumstances over which we have no control, Mrs Langtry will not appear this evening. We will see to your refunds as you depart, and again my apologies."

Holmes was among the first to exit, with Watson close behind. "Now there will be the devil to pay," said Watson. What am I to do if she has disappeared? They will revoke my bond."

The following days were most uncomfortable for

Watson. The local newspaper featured a fiery editorial denouncing *Brits* who come to America and try to get away with murder. "We put an end to that practice in 1776."

Mrs Hobson informed him she feared being accused of harboring a criminal. She gave Watson a week's notice, adding: "The better if sooner."

Watson no longer went walking as he was subject to grim stares, and parents led their children across streets to avoid him.

At loose ends and feeling abandoned by Sherlock, he called at the police station. The desk sergeant asked if he had come to confess.

"Not at all. I have come to ask if you are looking into the disappearance of William Yates, the butler. He may have evidence of significance in this case."

"Oh, now your lordship is advising the police on criminal investigation. Trying to pin it on the butler, are you? Well, let me tell you something, mister – butlers in Saratoga Springs do not commit murders. That is strictly a British activity."

"Nonsense," said Watson. "Besides, surely you must know that Mrs Langtry is British. And Yates is Irish. What do you make of that?"

"It sounds like a case for Constable Mulligan. You can share your concerns with him." He gestured with a thumb toward a comrade slumbering in a nearby chair. Watson recognized the officer who had challenged him upon arrival.

Mulligan, his blue uniform jacket unbuttoned and askew and his pot-like helmet on the floor at his side, sat, or more exactly sprawled, with his short salt-and-pepper beard buried in his chest and arms folded across a nourished midriff.

"Excuse me, sir," said Watson, standing before the drowsing officer.

Obtaining no response, Watson tapped the fellow on the shoulder. The constable started like a frightened deer, a wild look in his eyes.

"Begging your pardon, officer, I am wondering if you have looked into the possibility that Mrs Langtry's butler, Yates, may be involved in the murder of which I am accused."

"You're the rascal I've been watching, found at the scene," Mulligan snorted. "Don't bother me looking for scapegoats." As though he had resolved the matter, he eased back into a comfortable position, obviously about to resume his interrupted nap.

"If you are not interested in Yates, perhaps it would arouse your investigative interests to know that Col Sebastian Moran is in your midst. He is not the sort to do credit to your community, officer, and you would be wise to keep a sharp eye on him."

Mulligan frowned. "Is this the pot accusing the kettle? At this particular time of year, mister, you've got every conniver, grifter, card sharp and pickpocket in the country converging on Saratoga Springs for the racing season, and half of them putting on airs and calling themselves duke or colonel or railroad king. This Moran has caused no problems and has not come to our attention. You're on a lark and disturbing my rest."

"I happen to know that Moran is an assassin and that law enforcement officials in my home country are eager to see him brought to ground."

"Is this another of your tales, Dr Watson-masquerading-as-Watkins? Yes, I am well aware, you're that scribbler who writes up the adventures of the great Sherlock Holmes, whose unfortunate demise I have read about. He had a rather low opinion of those of us in public service who pound the beat and do the dirty work, did he not? And now it seems you are out to fill his shoes. Well, best to find yourself some legitimate occupation is my advice. There might be some work in the stables. Ask around back."

"You are a most uncooperative fellow," Watson proclaimed. "I hope you are not typical of the American constabulary."

"And I would hope you are not typical of visitors from merry old England, feeling free to murder whom you please here in our fair city."

Watson marched from the station feeling considerable agitation. He longed to show Mulligan and his lot a thing or two by applying tricks of the trade learned from Sherlock. He returned the glares of passerby on the street, alert for miscreants, scoundrels and villains. He hoped he might lay hands on a major personality of the criminal element and, as his reward, demand that Constable Mulligan be put to work mucking stables.

In such a mood he wandered front streets, side streets and parks, pavilions, piazzas and promenades, past steaming baths, mineral water fountains, statuary and monuments. He met only the accusative stares of passerby; no nefarious activities came to his attention. As the lunch hour passed, the Broadway corridor filled with holiday visitors dressed in the most lavish apparel. This was the afternoon fashion parade, a daily routine in which the ladies – nearly matched by the gents – displayed the latest in expensive custom apparel acquired from the many luxury shops lining the main street, or, like as not, imported from one of the world's great fashion centers. It was not only a foot parade –- the street filled with elegant coaches, some pulled by four or six high-stepping thoroughbreds, along with surreys, sulkies, broughams, buckboards and buggies. Watson found it difficult not to be judgmental, observing how participants would actually pause and applaud each other's displays of finery.

Along with the fashion parade, the sidewalks abounded with street entertainers such as acrobats, jugglers, musicians, and food and novelty vendors. And there were assorted beggars, from the blind man with his cup to ancient Civil War veterans whose placards announced what limb they had lost at which battleground: *Arm at Antietam* or *Leg at Bull Run.*

The crowd even included a crusading preacher attended by a dozen or so grim congregants. The preacher provided a loud and provocative sermon from behind the mask of a large megaphone. He denounced gambling, foppery, whiskey, unescorted women, and an assortment of other follies.

A group of young lads stood in front of the preacher, taunting him: "Trogg, Trogg, croaks like frog!"

Watson despaired of keeping an eye on all the possible candidates for scrutiny; they numbered in the thousands. He settled for taking up a station in front of the broad piazza of the United States Hotel, attempting to pay no attention to strollers who gave him a wide berth. It was there that his attention was compelled by a classic cry for help: "My purse! Someone has stolen my purse!"

Watson, alive to opportunity, raced up the stairway to the scene of the crime, ducking under the thick velvet cord securing an exclusive section, there to find a young lady in great distress and a small crowd gathering around her. He ascertained that the thief was still at large and set about surveying the immediate premises for anyone who might appear to be out of place, an obvious intruder in the very refined environment.

Watson's attention was drawn to a fellow standing back somewhat from the crowd, exhibiting a look of nonchalant disdain, attired as might indicate a prosperous western rancher. Watson took it into his mind that this was one of the wild American breed known as a cowpoke, notorious for nefarious activities such as robbery of banks and trains. Surely, Watson deduced, this fellow had gambled away whatever stake had accompanied him to town and was now reduced to petty crime. Watson became convinced that the purse was concealed under the great round dome of the cowpoke's western-style hat.

Wishing to bring matters to a swift conclusion, Watson leapt upon the westerner, seizing him in a bear-hug. As he was announcing that he had the thief in hand, his opponent stomped Watson's foot with a boot heel. The pain affected Watson's grip and the westerner broke free. "Sorry, pardner, I'm already taken for this dance."

Despite his injury, Watson was about to spring on him a second time when his suspect spun around, colliding with a passing member of the dining staff. The waiter bore a large tray loaded with china and gleaming silver-covered dishes cleared from one of the luncheon tables. The tray and dishes clattered to the ground, causing shrieks and groans among the assembled patrons whose finery suffered in the splattering shower of debris.

Those whose attention was not focused entirely on their own misery noticed a most interesting result of the collision. The lid flew off one of the silver servers, revealing the missing purse.

At that point Constable Mulligan came puffing up the stairway to where several of the gentlemen present had taken hold of the thieving waiter. "Might have known you'd be involved here," Mulligan muttered upon noticing Watson. "If you're involved in this ruckus, I'll be on you like jam on a biscuit, Mr Amateur Detective!"

"You will find that I played a part in apprehension of the villain," Watson declared, "though the real hero is this fellow." He turned to introduce the westerner but found the man had departed.

"Did anyone get the name of the cowpoke?" Watson inquired of those holding the thief. "No," came the reply from a bystander. "He beat a hasty retreat when the officer arrived. His parting comment was, 'Time to burn the breeze!'"

Chapter Thirteen

As Watson recounted his adventure to Holmes, the great detective expressed admiration. "You did very well, identifying the westerner as an outlaw. As you have described him, I would venture that you have made the acquaintance of Robert Parker, more widely known as the famous Butch Cassidy. I had heard he has been sighted hereabouts."

"If he is an outlaw, why did he interrupt the theft of the purse?"

"He is an outlaw possessed of a moral code of sorts, Watson. No doubt it offended his sense of honor to see a lady deprived of her purse."

"But he is himself a robber."

"He is a man of bold projects and has no use for petty criminals."

"What brings him to Saratoga Springs, I wonder?"

"Money and horses, I would venture. He and his cohorts are known to spree in New York City after a successful robbery. Once they have unburdened themselves of the loot they are no doubt on the lookout for the next job. At this season in this town, opportunities abound. But we shall leave that matter to the constables and private security operatives,

Watson. We have our own fish to fry."

"More like a fish to catch," said Watson. "Has there been any word regarding the whereabouts of Lillie Langtry?"

"Had anyone seen her, certainly we would have heard. A woman of her beauty and character stands out like a crystal in a coal bin. She is the statue of a goddess come to life."

"Spoken as though you are preparing to memorialize her, Holmes. Surely it has not come to that. Perhaps she has left some clue at her estate. We are remiss not to investigate the possibility."

"Come along, then, I've had enough of your fretting, let us have a look."

At the conclusion of a brisk hike toward the outskirts of town they arrived at a stately mansion and walked up the lengthy, tree-shaded drive. At the massive front door, Sherlock made use of large brass knocker.

"There appears to be no one home. Of course there will be someone at the stables, but they are far on down that lane; we've not been noticed. It may be the maid's day off, and we know not what has become of Yates, the butler."

Watson, dejected, remarked that the visit had been a waste of time.

Sherlock wasn't listening. "These locks look formidable but they are child's play."

"Holmes, the world lost a burglar of considerable

talent when you chose a career on the right side of the law."

"The law does not always view me as being on the right side, Watson, and that view is not without substance, as our present activity illustrates."

With the door opened, Sherlock urged his companion toward the interior. "You had best reconnoiter, Watson, while I keep watch."

"Just what is it I am looking for?"

"Clues, Watson, clues. Anything out of the ordinary; signs of a struggle, a suicide note, the footprints of giant cave bears. Use your wits, man."

Watson entered through a grand foyer and wandered through elegantly furnished rooms nearly devoid of evidence of human use. At last he came to a book-lined library having the comfortable look of a drawing room or salon. There were busts on pedestals, whatnots crowded with framed pictures, a sofa that might have served as a small island, armchairs and footstools, and a center table holding a stereoscope.

To the rear of that room he observed an opening into a small office area. He first noticed a delicate desk, its fancy trim work done by a craftsman of olden times, probably French, apparently a student of wedding cakes. As evidence that the usual occupant of the cubbyhole put personal taste above what might please the eye of a discriminating visitor, a sturdy oak captain's chair sat incongruously before the fancy desk.

Watson's attention was drawn to a tall wooden file cabinet, his thought being that it might hold a trove of information, possibly some useful clue. He was abruptly reminded of an elementary tenet of detection; that being to use caution in entering a room. His advance in the direction of the file cabinet was interrupted by the jab of a pistol barrel at his back.

"Mind your manners and no one gets hurt. Take a seat, mister."

Watson did as bidden, allowing a look at his captor. He was tanned, by heritage as much as by exposure, with a neatly trimmed full moustache, slightly graying. He stood a head shorter than Watson and looked as solid as a stevedore, though his attire was more that of a businessman, a brown double-breasted suit and bowler. His demeanor was casual, as though this sort of encounter was not unusual in his line of work.

"That's a good sport. No need for any rough stuff. So, out with it. What's your racket, why are you prowling around?"

"I would be obliged if you would get that weapon out of my face. It makes it difficult for me to compose my thoughts."

"I'm not asking for compositions, mister. Give it to me straight, and be quick about it. What's your business here?"

"I was simply paying a call on Mrs Langtry. There

was no answer when I rang, so I grew concerned and thought I'd have a look about."

"Hog slops. You know very well she's missing. You're that British scribbler, a pal of …"

And thereupon came a voice from behind him. "Sherlock Holmes, sir. And I am armed and ready, so you would be advised to do as asked. Now, put down the pistol so we may have a civilized exchange."

Though still in disguise as the old professor, it was Holmes, pistol in hand.

"If this don't beat all," the other muttered, placing his weapon on the desktop. Sherlock stepped into the room as quietly as a poacher traversing a royal preserve. He pocketed the man's pistol.

"To continue the conversation from a slightly different perspective, who are you and what is your business?" asked Holmes.

"My name is Frank Saracino. I'm a private detective."

"You are a Pinkerton man, and your reputation is of being one their best operatives."

"Thanks for the compliment, I suppose, though it doesn't seem to apply under the circumstances."

"Now that we're through introductions, I don't mind returning your weapon if you are willing to discuss the situation in a cordial manner."

"Good as done, Mr Holmes. Well, my business is that I'm on the trail of the Hole in the Wall Gang, particularly two of the ringleaders, and I've been at it for a few years now, through Canada, Mexico, out to San Francisco and then back to New York City. Not to mention a great many points in between."

"Hole in the Wall," mused Holmes. "That would be the group also known as the Wild Bunch, sometimes running to a hundred members. You must be a very busy man."

"I'm not out to round up the whole lot; that's work for sheriffs and posses. My assignment is to call a halt, one way or the other, to the criminal activities of Butch Cassidy and the Sundance Kid. The rest of them come and go – and mostly go because they're not as smart as the ring-leaders."

"Their exploits do make the British press now and then," Holmes said. "There is a romantic fascination with outlaws on horseback. I believe they are seen as some sort of populist rebels, not unlike our own legendary Robin Hood."

Watson seemed less than convinced of the Pinkerton's credibility. Though Holmes had earlier addressed the question, he asked Saracino: "The last stop you mentioned was New York City and I have to wonder, what in the world would western outlaws be doing there?"

Saracino looked bemused. "Well, mister, think about it. Robbing trains, stagecoaches and banks, stealing horses by the herd, it's not a hobby with them, you know. They do it for the money. And why do they want money? Characters like that, they want it to spend on a good time. As it happens, the big city has a lot more to offer than some shabby, slapped-together cow-town."

"Yes, I follow that. But then, what would bring them to Saratoga?"

"I was closing in on Butch and Sundance there in the city but their money ran low and they cleared out of town. We've got informants and the word was that they headed this way. This being where you find the finest horses in the country, it made some sense to me. They've run a herd of horses from Canada clear down to Mexico, so I guess New York to their Hole in the Wall hideout in Wyoming would not be too much challenge."

Holmes glanced around the little cubbyhole office. "And what brings you to our present situation, Mr Saracino?"

"Curiosity, that's all. I saw where Lillie Langtry disappeared. I've been keeping my eye on places that have big cash flow, hotels, gambling dens, the local branch of Tiffany's. When I saw Mrs Langtry was missing, I got to wondering what kind of ransom someone of her fame and connections would bring."

"So you dropped by to see if there might be a ransom note tacked to the door."

"Something like that."

Holmes seemed not quite convinced. "And it has nothing to do with the death of Pettigrew?"

"What would make you think so?"

"Nothing of great substance, at least not for the moment. Pettigrew's activity traces to the missing butler, Yates. Yates is an Irishman and that is a characteristic of the Molly Maguires secret society."

"You're far afield on that one. And it's a matter you would be wise to let drop, Mr Holmes. You're on the wrong side of us as it is over that *Valley of Fear* business."

Holmes drew up at the perceived affront. "I hold Watson the yarn-spinner accountable for that. It was never my intention that the tale be told."

Watson slapped the desk top. "Holmes, I have apologized for that one, time and again. I have written to the Pinkertons, father and sons, all to no avail because they do not answer."

Holmes pointed an accusing finger. "You made them out fools, now they take every opportunity to disparage me in the press. This country has no national police force; the Pinkertons are the guardians of Presidents, a position they do not like to see put in jeopardy, Watson." He took a deep breath and waved the matter aside. "At any rate, let it go. The war between the Pinkertons and an Irish anti-industrialist secret society is none of our concern."

"A wise observation, Mr Holmes. I'll be going now, if you don't mind. Nice to have made your acquaintance, and yours as well, Dr Watson. Could be our paths will cross again."

As Saracino departed, Watson said he probably

should have mentioned his encounter with Butch Cassidy.

"It is unlike an old soldier such as yourself to forget a cardinal rule of military training, Watson."

"And what is that?"

"Never volunteer. We have no reason to curry favor with the Pinkertons. Let us hold that information in reserve, it may be of use to us when, as Saracino suggests, our paths cross again."

"That seemed to me a first encounter," said Watson, "so I assume it was not Saracino following us during the course of your lecture on local architecture?"

"No, I think not. We are not his quarry; he is assigned strictly to the apprehension or destruction of the leaders of the Hole in the Wall Gang."

"So there are more Pinkerton agents about?"

As though stating a fact obvious to even the casual observer, Holmes said there were *dozens* more. "They handle security for the track, and I am sure for many of the wealthy patrons as well. Additionally, they supplement the incomes of a great many servants, bellhops, carriage drivers, tradesmen and, of course, the local police as informants. But they are not serious investigators, Watson. They need to advance beyond pummeling and shooting it out with every suspect. I would even suggest they might benefit from a reading of your somewhat sensationalized accounts of my more scientific methods."

In the aftermath of the excitement, Watson's mood had become subdued. "Well, I am sorry if the *Valley of Fear* tale has brought this situation on. If it were my purpose to intentionally capitalize on tales you wanted kept off the record, certainly I could make a fortune from the popular press right at this very moment. But the thought never crossed my mind. I believe I have demonstrated my willingness and ability to keep a confidence."

"Indeed you have, my dear friend. Let us wipe the slate clean and concentrate on the matter at hand."

On a table in the larger room Holmes noticed a book, the recently published *Master of Ballantrae* by the Scottish author Robert Louis Stevenson. He picked it up and began thumbing through it.

Watson scowled. "This is hardly the time for novels, Holmes."

"It is not so much the novel as the marginalia that I find interesting. Apparently Lillie took this fictional work for a real story of a treasure hunt in this region."

"What do you suppose prompted that strange idea?"

"As with this fellow Stevenson, she has probably heard tales based on the Scottish mariner Henry Sinclair's search for Viking treasure on these shores."

"Really? I know nothing of it."

"An adventure which took place a good many years before the much-celebrated Christopher Columbus so much as set sail. Well, of course, the

America's were a crossroads since ancient times, often visited by travelers and traders from afar. It merely happened that Columbus was far more successful at recording and promoting his adventures. But in this case, Sinclair's trip was recorded and charted by his pilot, Antonio Zeno. But Zeno hadn't the audience available to the Columbus expedition, so historians of the mainstream largely ignore it." Holmes held the book under Watson's nose. "Here, you see, she made a note of those who might help her find the treasure. She went to a wealthy acquaintance, Richard Canfield, thinking he might provide assistance. His name is familiar to me from the newspapers, he has gambling interests and spends considerable time here in Saratoga Springs. It is thought he may purchase the local casino, in which he is heavily invested."

"Surely," said Watson, "Mrs Langtry has far better ways of seeking wealth than to go off on some foolhardy treasure hunt."

Holmes cocked his head in disagreement. "She may have tired of the limelight, and may have fears of losing the charm that has thus far brought wealthy admirers to her doorstep. She is termed an adventuress in the popular press, a label meant to imply she is some sort of courtesan. But it may be more fitting in the purest sense of the word. Knowing Lillie, I imagine a treasure hunt would indeed have great appeal."

Chapter Fourteen

Later that day, Watson noticed Holmes again prepared for an outing. "I think there may be some benefit in contacting Lillie's friend, Richard Canfield. He is returning from an art-buying trip to Paris, according to the newspapers. I am on my way to the casino in which he has an interest, in the hope of an interview. And you?"

"Me? What on earth could I do?"

"As you may have noticed, we are attempting to favorably resolve the charge of murder hanging over your head. It seems the matter may be linked in some way to the amulet, which in turn is linked in some way to a treasure. If we can find the treasure, perhaps we can sit there, spiders in a web, awaiting the arrival of the actual murderer. Surely you follow my line of thinking?"

"Yes, but how will I assist in finding the treasure?"

"Since Mrs Langtry apparently thought there were clues in the book, *Master of Ballantrae*, it might do well to peruse it. But then, having an inclination toward fiction, perhaps you have already done so?"

"I take that as an unjust jab at my accounts of your adventures. But that aside, no; though I enjoy

Stevenson's adventure stories, that is one I have not read."

"Well, you know how I feel about fiction. I have no time for it. From the newspapers, though, I have noted that it was written while the author took the tuberculosis cure at Saranac Lake, up in the Adirondack mountains. It is certainly admirable that he managed to pile together so many words under severe winter conditions. As I understand it, he held forth in a drafty cabin in temperatures that at times reached forty below zero. He attributed his survival to tobacco and whiskey."

"Forty below," repeated Watson. "Little wonder he now resides in the tropical South Seas. And you suspect *Ballantrae* contains some clues regarding a treasure?"

"That is so, according to the reviews. Which, by the way, have been largely negative, the book was not received with great enthusiasm by those unfamiliar with Scots dialect."

"I don't know that it will be my cup of tea either; Scots is a difficult language hatched of sheep bleats and storm sounds."

"Now, there is a cure for boredom if I ever I heard one, Watson. Simply issue that assessment in a highland pub late one evening. But meanwhile, have a go at *Ballantrae*, will you?"

In later conversations, some details emerged about Sherlock's visit to the casino. He knew it to be likely closed at the hour of his visit, operations usually commencing along in the evening and carrying on late into the night, but thought the management might be on duty.

The casino was a formidable three-story edifice of orange brick; it might have been taken for a bank or other institution seeking to present a solid, fortress-like appearance. "It looked as though a tornado could hit it and bounce off," Holmes recalled. Though the building was closed, he proceeded up the short, steep front stairway and peered in through the glassed doorway.

He was followed up the stairway by a portly, clean-shaven gentleman who displayed a key while advising: "Closed until this evening, sir. I do hope you will come back then."

Holmes bowed slightly in greeting. "I am seeking an interview with the proprietor. Might that be you?"

"He's over at the track, where the action is at this hour."

"I suspect he does not hand out keys for the asking. You are an associate?"

"Yes, but it is Albert Spencer you want to see, whatever you're selling."

"This isn't a sales call. I was given the name of Richard Canfield by Mrs Lillie Langtry. He is not the owner?"

"I'm Canfield, and no, I'm not the owner yet. If Lillie sent you, I suppose you're on some crusade or other. I haven't got time right now, and assuming it's money you're after, I'm short of that as well."

Holmes, in his role as the elderly professor, drew himself up and arched an eyebrow. "I am a professor of art history. I was told of your interest in Edgar Degas, particularly his racecourse paintings. I am at work on a book on the Impressionist school and I have come a long way in the hope of conversing with you about it."

"Is that a fact? Well, I've nothing to show you here because my collection is down in the city."

"The city?"

"When folks around here talk about the city, mister, there's only one it could be, and that's New York City."

"I was not so much interested in seeing the paintings as in obtaining your views on Degas."

"All right, come along then." Canfield opened the brass-adorned door and led the way. The public gaming rooms were huge, the size of ballrooms, elegantly carpeted with fabric-draped windows as tall as the cathedral ceilings. There were no furnishings beyond the long tables where, later on, clusters of players would face the dealers over rising and falling piles of chips.

Ushering Holmes to a chair in a cozy sitting room adjacent a lengthy bar, Canfield fixed him with a sleepy-eyed, thoughtful look. "Professor, I am indeed impressed that you know of my interest in the Impressionist school of art. However, if you are a professor of art history, I am Ludwig of Bavaria. What is your game?"

"May I ask the basis of your conclusion?"

"Call it an educated guess. I have been a collector of art, in my own small way, long enough that even I know that most collectors are ignoramuses when it comes to art. They rely on dealers or academics, as you purport to be, as knowledgeable resources. So, chances – and I do know something about chances – are nine out of ten that a genuine professor would not so much as cross the street to discuss art with a collector. It goes, you see, the other way about."

Holmes pouted as might a child caught at the cookie jar. "I do see, and I am for once put in my place, that being that I am a private detective. My name must remain unbeknownst for now. Your cooperation will assure that as far as I am concerned, this conversation never took place."

"It might never take place regardless, mister. Why should I cooperate?"

"I am looking into the disappearance of Mrs Lillie Langtry and the murder of her chef. It has come to my attention that she had approached you recently regarding a treasure hunt. Apparently you rejected her proposal, seeing as a man in your position, with the eyes of the community focused on his activities, cannot afford association with a seemingly eccentric project. I have her note with your name and the name of one other possible sponsor on it; of course, there is no need that it come to the attention of the press."

Canfield gave a quick nod. "Now we are getting somewhere. There is hint of blackmail in what you say. But I may, in order to get you out of my hair, tell you what little I know. Should my name come up in any public discussion of this matter I will have your hide. You are quite right, in my position I cannot afford any association with such nonsense. And that, in conclusion, is exactly what I told Mrs Langtry in regard to her request for assistance."

"Why did she come to you?"

"We are friendly acquaintances. She was under the misapprehension that my occupation, proprietor of several gambling enterprises, meant that I would gladly join her in a risky venture. The fact is, I cater to risk-takers but am myself quite conservative in business matters. And I would not jeopardize my intention to buy out Mr Spencer by becoming identified in some hare-brained treasure hunt."

"Entirely understandable," Holmes said. "Perhaps you can assist with some information, though. The other name on her notepad was Angus McSnay. But I came to you because it was an easy matter to locate you; I know nothing of this McSnay. Do you?"

"Oh, a bit. He's a new man in town, calls himself Captain McSnay. He set up in a fancy steam yacht out on the lake, high stakes private game. Nothing legal about it, but certain parties are paid off so they look the other way. Do you mean to tell me she went to him for help? That's like … it's like a cow handing a knife to the butcher."

"I hope she has not made such a mistake, Mr Canfield. Could you describe this Captain McSnay?"

"Tall, bordering on gaunt, a fierce, weathered face, graying but in that dignified way that adds rather than detracts. A commanding sort, probably not one to do battle with on his own field, though it may come to that."

"Yes, that fits with my suspicions. What exactly do you mean, it may come to that?"

"This is totally confidential, you understand? I tell you only because it may help illuminate the situation regarding Mrs Langtry. If she went to McSnay, she is in bad company. The thing is, I sent a couple of tough cowboys from out West to hire on with McSnay as crew. These boys are experts at the rough and tumble, and eager for a quick dollar."

"You infiltrated, and then?"

"I'm not running a tea parlor here, mister. If McSnay thinks he can siphon off business from this place, he's going to have cause to think again. When I give the word, those boys I sent over will bust up his game, and no doubt fill their pockets with his profits. That's how I deal with shady racketeers who move in on me."

"You may face more of a challenge than you imagine. If you are dealing with the man I believe McSnay to be, he is no ordinary crook."

"Don't worry, mister. The fellows I sent over aren't ordinary cowboys, either."

Chapter Fifteen

Near noon that day, as Watson was perusing the Stevenson novel, there came a knock at his door. It was Holmes. "Have you seen the newspaper?"

Watson shook his head. "No, I haven't been out. Mrs Hobson seems to have relented about ousting me from my quarters. She brought a fine breakfast and I have been reading. Come in, she just brought a fresh pot of coffee."

"Have a look." Holmes handed him the paper.

One full column was a second-day story on the disappearance of Lillie Langtry, adding much speculation to the few facts. It was suggested that, being a theatrical person, she might at the moment be resting in a sanitarium under the care of medical professionals. Another conjecture was that she had run off with a wealthy admirer and was happily ensconced in one of the manors, estates or great lodges in the region. The story then digressed into a critique of her acting ability, followed by remarks on her wardrobe.

"You might note the segments of the story that I have marked; they seem the reporter's few efforts to rise above the sensational. There is, though, very little to satisfy the scientific mind in search of facts."

Watson scanned the article. "I note the suggestion that she has run off with one of her rich admirers, an action she has apparently found appealing in the past. Do you think that likely?"

Holmes frowned, not so much in skepticism as in thought. "I can see how they come by the theory. Look around this town, Watson. I'm sure you will notice how some of the most respected captains of international industry, paragons of marital virtue in their home communities, become gallivanting bachelors the moment they are on the loose in Saratoga Springs. They have so-called cottages provided by the hotels for their convenience, they have townhouses, they have boat houses, and they even have little private villages out in the mountain wilds called lodges and camps."

"We will never find her."

"I beg to disagree. If she is in an inhabited area, any one of a legion of sportsmen, loggers, prospectors and other inhabitants would recognize her."

"How so?"

"The walls of cabins and shanties throughout the backwoods, wherever men are deprived of feminine contact, are undoubtedly pinned up with likenesses of her. There would be no need for a missing person poster in her case."

"If she is not keeping company with a wealthy admirer, where is she?"

"I do not know, of course. Interestingly, the press hasn't tied her disappearance to the murder of Pettigrew. Given the penchant for the sensational it is a wonder they haven't suggested she killed him in a lover's quarrel and is hiding out in that western outlaw den, the Hole in the Wall."

"I suppose it is possible."

"If one believes the press, Watson, it is possible that our planet is about to be invaded by giant cave bears coming to steal our cabbages. Without data we cannot dismiss the idea entirely, but for all of what may be termed her faults, I do not see Lillie as a murderess."

"I am inclined to agree with you. Well, then, what are we to do about locating her?"

"She is free to come and go as she pleases, Watson. It may be, as suggested, she is simply in the midst of some affair, creating more mischief for the press to dwell upon. Scandals follow her like dogs follow a meat wagon."

"Holmes, though you often assert and evidence a lack of emotional involvement in human affairs, I am beginning to believe your pique over how matters turned out between you and Mrs Langtry has biased your approach to a very serious matter."

The great detective looked at Watson as though he were a museum curiosity. "I can understand how your appetite is whetted by the possibility of sensational material for future tales, Watson, but pray restrain yourself. I refrain from public activity because I am incognito, as you are supposed to be, and besides, we are guests in this country and must conduct ourselves with some reserve. We cannot dash madly into this case. We need facts."

"These facts, are they to materialize from thin air?"

"I have interviewed Canfield with mixed results, basically confirming that Moran is indeed operating in the area. What do you suggest we do? Peer into abandoned wells, poke about in the lofts of old carriage houses, troll the lake with grappling hooks, interview every vagrant, every Indian, every gypsy, waif and stray for miles around? I am awaiting the answer to a telegram, at which point I will decide on a further course of action. Attend to your studies for now. I will call again in a few hours."

The telegram Sherlock referred to was sent to me in London. You may recall that the mystery of the missing amulet first came to light when a visiting professor had asked to see it. Now, Sherlock was asking the name of the professor. I inquired of the curator of the royal collections and learned that it was – as I suppose Sherlock suspected – the since-deceased Professor James Moriarty.

Loathe though I am to stray from my beaten paths, at Sherlock's request I made straight for Moriarty's now-abandoned lair and secured every shard and scrap of paper I could lay hands on. Sure enough, among the notes was a copy of memorandum to Moran from Moriarty concerning the amulet. It was made with carbonated paper, indicating that the original had been sent to Moran.

My Dear Moran,

It has come to my attention that a certain amulet, of some value as an antiquarian collectible but having rather more value to us as, shall I say, a bargaining chip, is missing from the royal gem collection.

My research indicates that this amulet, in the shape of a Viking axe with a bear's head for decoration, is now in the possession of the entertainer Lillie Langtry.

Rumor on the academic whisper-circuit is that the amulet holds the key to a great treasure. Whether that is so or not, I am further given to understand that it was presented to Mrs Langtry by Prince Albert Edward on impulse; he had no right to do so. He has been ordered to retrieve it.

Obviously, whoever possesses the amulet possesses a power over Albert Edward, and perhaps the key to a great treasure. Need I say more?

Most Sincerely (and etc).

Informed of my discoveries, Sherlock continued his investigation. *What follows is his account of his findings:*

"I called at Lillie Langtry's home again, this time encountering the maid, who had been with her for many years, attending to her chores. At first she would not open the door, but I allowed her to see through my professorial disguise and she then recognized me from my stay in Monaco. I went straight to the heart of the matter, asking if she had any observations regarding the theft of Mrs Langtry's jewelry."

The maid told Sherlock she had more than suspicions; she had knowledge. She said both she and Yates, the butler, were certain the thief was the chef, Pettigrew. Yates, asking around, had discovered that Pettigrew was a regular customer at the casino until expelled for unpaid debts. Through further inquiries among local gossips, it was learned that McSnay then sought out Pettigrew and invited him to join the clandestine gambling party on his steam yacht on the lake. In short order Pettigrew was again racking up a large debt. So, said she, Yates concluded that Pettigrew was stealing jewelry to pay his losses. There came a point where Pettigrew actually had the gall to compliment Mrs Langtry on a certain amulet in her possession and to ask permission to see the bauble.

Sherlock, coaxing the maid on with her tale, said that surely Mrs Langtry had better sense than to display it.

Hardly, said the maid. "You didn't know Pettigrew. To your face he was sweetness, a mewing pussycat, but turn your back and he became a viper. He was constantly trying to shift blame for any misconduct to Mr Yates or myself. When found prowling areas of the house where he had no business, he would claim one or the other of us had sent him on an errand. Fortunately our standing with Mrs Langtry is such that his lies did no harm."

Sherlock asked if Pettigrew and Yates roomed on the premises. She said that was true of Yates, while Pettigrew resided elsewhere. He then asked to see Yates' room.

"The room was neat as pin," Sherlock recalled. "It might have been a hotel room awaiting the next guest, but for clothing and a very few personal items. However, among those few items was a journal, and I perused it with interest. The entries were in a code, kabalistic and, given my studies in that area, easily translated. A strange document, it told of a special edition of a book, *Justine et Juliette*, by the Marquis de Sade. This bizarre literary freak is bound, so it is claimed in certain secretive circles, in the skin of female breasts."

"Good heavens, Holmes," gasped Watson. "Surely

such things cannot be."

"There are those among us, Watson, whose sensitivities are not as delicate as your own. There is, for instance, a longstanding tradition of binding trial documents in the skin of executed murderers. You would find my monograph on the subject most enlightening, I am sure, but unfortunately I have none of my papers at hand."

"Such studies are not a decent pursuit for a gentleman, Holmes."

"Perhaps not, but I am a detective first and foremost. And were you to explore the subject as I have, you would learn that works of the *Justine et Juliette* sort are not always simple erotica. They may guard alchemical secrets or other coded materials."

Watson dismissed Sherlock's defense. "It is a disgusting pursuit. It amazes me, the sordid endeavors justified in the name of detection."

"Grist for your literary mill, Watson."

"There are limits, and books bound in human skin exceed those limits. I prefer not to dwell. What more did you learn at the Langtry residence?"

Sherlock said he next asked the maid when she had last seen either Yates or Pettigrew.

"I have found it strange, sir, that until this moment no one has asked. For some reason, on the night before that unfortunate man Watkins was arrested for the murder, Pettigrew fled the house in a great hurry, without having prepared the evening meal. And then

Mr Yates was off, apparently in pursuit. It was two days later, after Mrs Langtry's exchange of notes with you, Mr Yates returned, looking quite a bit worse for whatever misadventure had ensued.

"At about that time a boy arrived bearing a note. I only caught a glance at it but can tell you it was signed by Reverend Trogg. Shortly thereafter, Mrs Langtry and Yates were off in the wagon. I have seen neither since, and they left no word as to their destination."

Upon learning the whereabouts of Pettigrew's lodging, Sherlock paid a visit. It turned out to be little more than a stable where cots are rented out in shifts.

"The landlady, a ferocious old harridan who took me immediately for a snoop, proved most uncooperative until she focused in on the several silver dollars I held in my palm. Suddenly she became a model of cooperation. She not only knew Pettigrew but had a box of his belongings in keeping.

Most interesting was a note:

> *Time is up, Pettigrew! Retrieve the amulet*
> *or learn to swim wearing a cement*
> *overcoat! Last warning.*

Chapter Sixteen

It may not be necessary to note again for the benefit of you, the reader, that this account is a compendium of bits and pieces, for the most part based on conversations with my brother and Dr Watson as well as upon reports from my operatives. In some instances I have had to resort to what a critic might term 'conjecture', though in my line it was known as 'informed speculation'.

I had always found interesting Sherlock's facility for character creation and it was over dinner some years later that I asked about the primary role he chose to play in Saratoga Springs, that of Professor Varner.

"If indeed you were researching Norse sagas, Sherlock, I find that very unlike you. It has been your contention that you collect only such knowledge as is useful to you. How then do you justify that particular interest?"

"What I was researching, in particular, were treasure tales which have come down from the Norse, Mycroft. A few occur in sagas relating to travels to America. They are quite a justifiable study for a detective because, often enough, a buried or hidden treasure is a sign of grand theft. The two primary reasons that come to mind for hiding a treasure would be, first, to prevent its theft, but secondly, to secure stolen property."

"And the sagas provide clues to hidden treasures?"

"Indeed, the sagas indicate the distinct possibility that Viking exploration, perhaps even colonization, took place in what is now the northeastern United States, long before the celebrated arrival of Columbus or that of earlier visitors such as our fellow Scot, Sir Henry Sinclair. There are stories that they brought and buried pillaged treasures."

I was puzzled. "It is unusual, Sherlock, for you to be taken in by legends."

"Oh, I do not take them as gospel, Mycroft. But the sagas are, collectively, an early version of our encyclopedia, you might say."

"And so they are credible?"

"Not entirely. They are tales. But then, look at the Encyclopedia Britannica of a century ago. We chuckle over some of the entries because they are so outlandish. But they state facts as perceived at the time, and therefore warrant study for the truths they may contain."

"And what did you learn?"

"As a matter of fact, I produced a monograph on the subject. I believe I can quote a passage from memory: 'A savage Viking cult, the Berserkers, may have attempted to settle on the North American continent. They were the terror of their enemies owing to do-or-die ferocity, fueled by mead and hallucinogenic mushrooms. The Berserkers also became quite unpopular among fellow Vikings, as they were prone to attack their own kind as readily as foe. Legend has it that the Berserker group in Scotland was driven out by their Norse neighbors who had settled there, and they sailed away, taking along a hoard of treasure. Where they went is not known. However, the exodus occurred at about the time when, according to the sagas, the Norse were prowling the coast of America.'"

"That certainly is a vague account."

"Well, Mycroft, let me ask you this. If you possessed a king's ransom that needed to be hidden somewhere, would you subsequently advertise its location to the world at large?"

"Not likely. And there was indeed a treasure?"

"In legend, the hoard consisted of silver and gold ingots, bracelets, brooches, chains, rings and other jeweled ornaments, as well as coins, gathered from wherever the Berserkers looted and plundered – Africa, Asia, all corners of Europe."

"I have heard nothing of that. I am, however, familiar with tales of American Indian cities of gold. Did your treasure interests involve those rumors?"

"Some of the searchers have been of the belief that one of the lost cities, Norumbega, lies in the area now known as upstate New York, along the far reaches of the Hudson River. At least one account refers to it as the northern El Dorado. There are standing stones in the region which believers take to be of Viking making, but to mainstream science they are identified as natural geologic formations. There are accounts of a magnificent city among reports of early French explorers, though they conflict as to its whereabouts. It has been proposed that Norumbega is the Indian remembrance of the name Norvega, for Norway, given by Vikings. Thus they would have named the city after their homeland."

"It seems to me rather thin soup, Sherlock."

"Indeed. Which is what led me take the matter up with those most likely to know."

But let us return to the situation in Saratoga Springs, where we observe another meeting of Sherlock and the doctor.

Watson looked up from the book he was studying. Based on a reading of *Master of Ballantrae* he had visited *The Literate Mallard* and acquired several more volumes in pertinent areas of geography and history. "What have you learned, Watson?"

"In conversation with your friend Sophie I learned that the melancholy poet Edgar Allen Poe resided near here while working on his poem, *The Raven*."

"Fascinating. Anything of use at the moment?"

"I think it says much of this area that Poe found inspiration here. However, what else? From the

Ballantrae novel I learned that whiskey is a false consoler."

"Well, I would hope you take that message to heart. But I meant, what have you learned regarding the whereabouts of the treasure which we assume Mrs Langtry to be pursuing?"

"I have learned that there is clear sailing from the mouth of the Hudson all the way to Albany, so a Viking ship could navigate that distance. And Albany was the initial destination of the *Ballantrae* adventurers. They then traveled sixteen hours further. At a marching pace they might travel eighty miles in sixteen hours. So the treasure lies eighty miles north of Albany."

"Excellent, Watson. Except that it would be a wonder if they made half that distance, given the lack of roads at the time. There would have been only Indian trails, difficult to follow. You have made a mistake in putting it too far afield."

"And so, where do you put the treasure, Holmes? Stevenson locates it in the mountains near a lake. That could describe a large portion of New York State."

"If my thinking is correct, Watson, the treasure, if such exists, could actually be not so very far from us here in Saratoga Springs. To the north and west you encounter mountains after short travel, and there are highland lakes to be found, not large ones but lakes nonetheless. But access must require possession of the amulet, for some reason. The maid said Lillie received a communication from that fellow Trogg, so we may assume she has gone to meet with him, no doubt in hope of securing the amulet. We may find her if we can locate his remote castle."

"May I suggest the fellow who brought me here from Lake George, Jack Thibedeau, might serve as a guide, or at least recommend someone reliable. He is leader of an Indian encampment located on the outskirts of town."

"A grand suggestion, Watson! Let us be off!"

Chapter Seventeen

On the fringe of town there was an Indian encampment, not an official reservation of course, not so near the grand avenues, great hotels and mighty mansions of the wealthiest enclave north of New York City. Fine that the Indians might be given a home in some place of no economic value, but not here. However, it was accepted that the Indians were an exotic draw and so they were allowed temporary settlement on a few vacant lots, a camp during the tourist season. They were welcome only as a summer sideshow. After that they would be advised to make tracks back to their official reservation on the Canadian border, or to find themselves treated no differently than gypsies and tramps.

Did the tourists, seeing the tipis and lean-tos, believe they were visiting a genuine Indian village? It would be hard to say. Certainly most Europeans knew next to nothing of how Indians lived since they were driven off to remote locations by advancing settlers and other land-grabbers. And perhaps the tourists would be fooled by place names, the names the Indians left behind when pushed out, Saratoga and Adirondack and a hundred more, as if these were evidence that those who gave the names were yet around. For example, Saratoga Springs lies not far from the Mohawk River, but you would be hard pressed to find any Mohawks along that river – it had become the engine of miles and miles of factories and mills.

The residents of this particular encampment, Jack Thibedeau's relations, were remnants of the Mohawk tribe. Not long ago, as part of a greater group, the Iroquois Confederacy, they ruled for hundreds of miles in the region. And, yes, it had been none other than Sir William Johnson, the agent of King George, who deprived these people of their lands. Perhaps better the land traded to him for at least a pittance than taken with guns by the exploitative hordes that followed.

There were few other visitors when Sherlock and his companion arrived at the encampment's carnival strip, an arcade of bright awnings featuring handicrafts for sale, decorated baskets, beadwork and blankets hanging on display around booths of rough timber and scrap lumber. Other souvenirs and trinkets decorated the interiors of the booths. Costumed barkers in headdresses and fringed leather suits hawked games of chance. One had to look back behind the midway to see the residential side of the encampment, the lean-tos and tents of the nomadic concessionaires.

"These people do have a fondness for games of

chance," Watson said as the pair made their way toward the midway.

"Indeed," agreed Holmes. "It would be a small justice if one day they owned the casinos that are now in the hands of the Canfields of this world."

A man in beaded leather wearing a feathered headdress hurried up to them. "Welcome to our humble campground, gentlemen. I am Chief Swift Moose."

"You are Jack Thibedeau," said Watson.

"Oh, it's you, Dr Watkins. What a pleasure. And you have brought a friend."

Watson introduced Holmes, as Professor Varner.

"Gentlemen, you are just in time to witness one of our grand sporting events, and you are most welcome to wager upon the outcome. Step right this way."

They followed Thibedeau under a banner announcing: 'Amazing Famous Flaming Arrow Exhibition!' A small group of Indian youngsters sat around in a circle in a clearing behind the midway arcade. In the center of the circle were laid out a bow and arrow. Some distance away, at the far end of the clearing, loomed a giant old oak tree.

"This is quite a simple game," Thibedeau said. "From a branch on yonder oak tree hangs an apple on a string. You see? As a target, it is very near invisible, I think you would agree. So, in this game, the apple will be set in motion. Now, here we have the young braves of our tribe, gathered in powwow. They are calling upon the powers that be – the sun, the wind, the ancestors – seeking guidance. Why? Because one of these young braves, one that you shall choose, is going to attempt to shoot an arrow and hit that apple. Not just any arrow, either, but a flaming arrow. What do you think? Can he possibly succeed?

"Sometimes," Thibedeau continued, "on very rare occasions, the apple has actually been hit. Personally, I would bet a little bit that he can hit it. And I would bet a lot that he cannot. After all, this is not a stationary apple like the one in your William Tell story. This is a swinging apple. Now, you are probably wondering, why, if there is hardly a chance of success, do we accept your bet against our young brave? Well, this is an ancient ritual, you see. We want to preserve the old ways. If by chance the young brave does hit the apple, we will give him the feather of an eagle to wear. So, you see, our bets really have nothing to do with him. They are between us."

Much to Watson's chagrin, Holmes seemed intrigued. Watson took his elbow and steered him to one side. "This is some sort of scheme, can you not see that?"

"Of course it is, but we must build rapport, Watson. Play along, if you don't mind." Holmes turned back to Thibedeau. "Suppose I told you I can make that shot, blindfolded?" Holmes asked.

"Suppose I told you I am *Atenenyarhu,* the giant man-eating monster? Meaning I seriously do not believe you."

Holmes smiled. "I propose to bet a ten dollar gold piece."

"Ten dollars?"

"Precisely."

"Blind-folded?"

"Absolutely."

"I will supply the blindfold. What you propose cannot be done."

Holmes turned to Watson. "I take you for a betting man, Watkins. Since I will be performing the feat, I think you should place the bet."

Watson raised his voice. "Varner, I have every confidence in your many abilities but I must say, you are bluffing in this case. You cannot possibly make the shot as you propose to do it."

"Oh, ye of little faith. Let me assure you, Watkins, that I am a good man with a longbow."

"That's as may be, but you have added a blindfold. You have taken this from the realm of archery into that of magic. But, very well, this is a betting town and I bow to the maxim, *when in Rome...*"

Holmes addressed Thibedeau: "Allow me a moment to inspect the target." He strode toward the oak tree, muttering to himself as he paced. He took the apple in hand, stood back a bit and released it, watching its arc.

Rejoining the group, he again spoke to their host: "If you would be so kind, when releasing the apple please stand where you saw me standing just then, and release it as I did — not a toss, you understand, just let it go."

"Done," declared Thibedeau. He took a bandanna from around his neck. "Here is your blindfold." He walked to the tree and grasped the apple. Holmes took up a bow and nocked an arrow. He put the blindfold in place, fully covering his eyes. One of the boys came forward to light the bit of oil-soaked rag at the tip of the arrow. "Ready," announced Holmes.

"Aiyee!" shouted Thibedeau, releasing the apple. He dove for cover behind the huge tree.

The flaming shaft hurtled straight and true.

It came remarkably close to the target, but it missed the apple by the merest fraction. Thibedeau removed the arrow from the tree and returned. "An incredible shot, sir. I am reluctant to take your friend's money after such a show. But I will take it, a bet is a bet."

"Of course you shall take it," said Holmes. "I missed my shot."

Watson shook his head. "I predicted as much. But I will say, you came closer than I could have imagined!"

"As close as need be."

As Watson was making good on his bet and puzzling over Holmes' strange remark, an eerie whistling sound pierced the air. Watson looked around for the source. "Whatever is that?"

"The signal," exclaimed Thibedeau. "It's our lookout alerting us to a police raid. Follow me and I'll get you out of here."

Holmes balked. "But there is an important matter we must discuss."

"It'll have to wait. They will arrest us for gaming."

Watson took his friend by the arm. "Let us go, Sherlock! The last thing I need is another arrest."

Thibedeau led the pair through a labyrinth of alleyways and sidestreets, emerging in a secluded grove overlooking Congress Park. There Holmes asked about his service as guide to Trogg's castle.

Thibedeau shrank back as though suddenly aware that Holmes carried an infectious disease. "That is a place of evil. It is taboo for my people. I cannot guide you."

"This matter may be of importance to the Bear Clan," said Holmes.

Thibedeau's features turned stony. "And why should that matter to me?"

Holmes raised a finger, pointing at the Indian's neck. "You wear a bear-claw necklace and you have a bear-paw tattoo. You say your father is a Frenchman but to the Iroquois it is the mother's side that controls identity. Now, I believe that an amulet of importance to your clan is to be found at the castle." Holmes went on to give a brief description of the amulet and its background. "You would not want it to remain in the wrong hands," he concluded.

"Then we must consult my grandfather, Owl Eyes. He is a powerful shaman and is not affected by the taboo. He has told me of secret tunnels that may prove useful. You will not find or even get near the place without help."

"And will he be willing to help us?" asked Sherlock.

"He is one of the last of the Guardians who wear such an amulet. He will want to assist in recovering the one you speak of."

Arrangements were made for a trip on the following day.

On the way back to their lodgings, Holmes and Watson in roles as Varner and Watkins stopped in at Johnny Sophie's bookshop where they heard news of the Rev Trogg. "He was in a state of extreme agitation," Sophie observed. "Asked if I knew of any bookbinders who might take a special commission."

"I don't care for the sound of that," said Sherlock. "We must make haste to look into this, I fear we will find Lillie transformed into a fine binding."

Watson frowned. "You might have better luck on your own."

"Nonsense. This is just the sort of adventure you need to restore your confidence. I must insist on your assistance. Besides, you have yet to venture into the mountains to our north and you are missing the highlight of the region."

Lost in reverie for a moment, Watson responded:

"Indeed, my appetite for a closer look at the Adirondacks was whetted by a visit to a gallery in the hotel where I first found accommodations. There were scenic depictions of wondrous vistas, idyllic camp settings, and wild beasts such as moose, panther and wolf. I was particularly taken by a Currier & Ives print, titled *Camping Out*, wherein hunters enjoy a visit to nature in the rough. And in the January edition of Harper's found in my room, there were wild Adirondack scenes by the artist, Remington."

Sophie commented: "Sorry to report, those illustrations are from a time gone past. There is little of the original wilderness left, most of it ravaged by loggers and miners, and the rest carved into private Great Camps of the rich, or hotels and clusters of cottages for the tourist. In every suitable locale you will find a grand hotel of hundreds of rooms with cleared grounds of thousands of acres.

"In addition, many an attractive natural setting has been adapted to industrial use, particularly along the rivers and streams, and communities have grown up around such mills and factories, pushing back the forest and its dwellers. Any good farmland, of which there was little in the first place, has long since been worked and exhausted, most farms are now abandoned. It may be that one day fresh wilderness will flourish where those vacant farms now stand."

Watson was not pleased. "You present a picture of devastation."

"Sad to say, that has been the way of the European expansion and exploitation," Sophie said. "The great forests are the enemy, savage realms to be subdued and put to work for our purposes. But the attitude is changing; the Adirondack region has been declared a preserve and soon will be named a state park. It will be huge, containing more than 100 mountain peaks."

Holmes proposed a compromise vision. "I would not doubt that we will see the most remote of the country, from what Thibedeau has said. At the higher elevations, ranging up to 5,000 feet, we may find a natural setting which the lumbermen have not taken down."

Watson patted his leg, injured long ago by a Jezail bullet. "I am not in the best condition for mountaineering."

"My dear friend, I recall how you kept pace in the heights of Switzerland. I will hold your hand if I must but you are most certainly coming along."

"There will be no need for hand-holding, Holmes. And, yes, it may be that this proposed adventure brings to mind that terrible time at Reichenbach. But, as you insist, I will join you."

And so the next day they joined Thibedeau in his wagon and set off to the mountains. As they climbed the long grade from the foothills on twisting trails, the Indian entertained them with anecdotes regarding catastrophic incidents. "This is the turn where Jake Southall's wagon went over." "Here's where a group of Tories fleeing from Albany froze to death." "There, a mining camp was devastated by forest fire and many of its inhabitants lost." And so on, much to Watson's discomfort.

The rutted road played out at the base of high ridge. "My grandfather does not make himself accessible to those who do not know the way," Thibedeau advised. "You are in country unknown to the average tourist who huddles beside the popular lakes. This is a taste of the Adirondacks of old."

Indeed it was so, a panoramic view of the mountains appeared as an ocean of flowing, towering green and brown swells, some yet capped in snowy white. Clouds hovered about the crests and at the highest points could be seen merged with the landscape, enveloping all in mist or fine rain. At nearly every turn of the rough, steep climb appeared some new lake, pond, river or stream, often lined with stately, spindly birches and robust maples. Thibedeau claimed there were thirty species of trees to be found in the region.

"The state has preserved a vast portion of the region," said Thibedeau.

"Yes," said Holmes, "our bookseller friend tells us it will soon officially become a huge park, amounting to about one-fifth of the land-base of the state."

Thibedeau's look swept the vast landscape below and before them. "This land should be returned to the original inhabitants who were deprived of it by fraud, trickery and whiskey. But at least it will be protected from the robber barons who act as laws unto themselves, bent on reducing all this to barren wasteland. They take what brings profit and then abandon it."

"It is now off limits to future development?" said Watson.

"It is a complicated arrangement. The park will be a sort of patchwork; the state will not acquire all the private land. Much of it is settled, there are many towns and other communities. The state still sells timber-harvesting rights. But a move is afoot to keep millions of acres forever wild, protected by law."

Leaving the wagon, they followed a narrow path, a comfortable carpet of humus, through a forest of firs. The air was sweeter, rich in the smell of forest and glade. The path took them along an awesome chasm, a river-carved pit so deep it seemed a gateway to the netherworld. Bluejays taunted and hawks circled above on the currents of mountain air. With Thibedeau leading the way, they climbed higher and higher, ultimately working their way through a thick tangle of highland brush.

"I am surprised that you are not averse to such heights after the experience at Reichenbach," Watson commented.

"Heights?" exclaimed Holmes. "Come with me to Tibet sometime, Watson. I will show you paths that would dizzy a mountain goat."

"My bad leg aches and my good leg is wearing out, Holmes. I prefer the avenues and level lanes."

Thibedeau waved them to silence. "Sekoh! Sekoh, yonkyatenron!" he called out. "I have told him I bring friends."

An old man emerged from a rough-hewn log hut. Dressed in a flannel shirt and denim pants, he was a wiry, leathery-looking fellow, as much a part of the woods as the trees and rocks. Thibedeau approached him and they spoke at length in Iroquois. He waved Holmes and Watson to approach and made introductions as Varner and Watkins. "I see who you are," said the old man, cryptically. "But I will abide by your game."

The old man listened as Holmes explained the situation as known to him. At the mention of the amulet, he showed a necklace beneath his shirt.

"The amulet," cried Watson, lunging for it.

Holmes intercepted him and pulled him away. "Calm yourself, man! That is similar to the one we seek but it is not it. It seems each of those assigned the role of Guardian possesses one. But note that it is iron, whereas the one we seek is silver."

Owl Eyes nodded. "If the lady is prisoner in the castle," he said, "you can perhaps reach her through secret tunnels known to me. I have spent much time in that area because, as a medicine man, it is my mission to cleanse it of evil."

Holmes frowned. "From what I hear, you haven't

exactly been successful."

"If my medicine could entirely cleanse this world of evil, what work would there be for you?"

Holmes, yet passing himself off as Varner, looked innocently off into the trees and made no comment.

It was decided that Thibedeau would borrow a pony and return to his camp for reinforcements while the grandfather escorted Holmes and Watson to the castle in the wagon.

Thibedeau set off: "Onen ki' wahi. Goodbye."

Chapter Eighteen

The old Indian had little to say as the wagon traversed a narrow and rutted mountain road, a maze of switchbacks, probably carved out for logging or mining. He merely hummed a monotonous three-note tune. They passed through a canopy of forest with an understory of brier, fern and laurel, a silent world but for the creaking clatter of the wagon. Watson commented on the condition of the road, which made for a bone-rattling travel experience.

"This would do as a carnival ride," said Watson.

"An old warpath," muttered the old man. "Few care to risk their lives to travel it today."

Holmes managed to engage the fellow in a bit of conversation which he summed up: "From his descriptions of people he has seen at the castle I recognized Benny Pearl, the desperate forger, and Maude Caulkins, the charming but homicidal daughter of the captain of the lost ship, Celestine. And I should also mention Womack, the political assassin. It seems Trogg is managing a hideout for the Moriarty gang, passing it off as a colony of innocent craftspeople."

The sky had darkened and the atmosphere turned

dank and musty. At a turn, Owl Eyes reined in the horses. "There is a man lying over there near the roadside. We must see to him."

At the injured man's side, Holmes identified him as Yates, the butler.

Yates was stretched out beneath a tree, his face ashen. Watson bent over him. "This man is comatose," said Watson. "There is nothing I can do. He must be conducted to a hospital."

Owl Eyes glanced at Yates and disappeared into the underbrush. He returned as Holmes and Watson were in the midst of discussing how to convey the patient to town. Owl Eyes lit a small fire and blew the resultant smoke into Yates' face.

"You'll choke him to death," exclaimed Watson.

"Leave the medicine man to his remedy. Civilization, so-called, has much to learn from healers who live close to the natural world," Holmes said.

Yates' eyes fluttered and his lips moved. "Tried to stop them. Trogg, he kidnapped Mrs Langtry. McSnay swung at me with his rifle-stock, that's the last I remember. You must save her."

"We will do our best," Sherlock assured him. At that, Yates closed his eyes again and seemed to fade from consciousness.

"He will sleep for a long time. That is best," said Owl Eyes.

"Let us make him as comfortable as possible," said Holmes

"I had the impression he was unknown to you. How is it you knew the man's name?" asked Watson.

"We find him on the path taken by Mrs Langtry and the butler, he wears a gray waistcoat with the tips of white cotton gloves showing from the pocket, his lapel pin bears the harp symbol of those who aspire to an Irish Free State – given his attire and the circumstances of the encounter, how could he be other than Yates, the butler?"

Holmes asked Watson if he would mind staying with Yates.

Watson, having been wary of the castle trip all along, readily agreed.

I would, of course, have diverted agents of my own to assist my brother and his companions had I been aware of their situation. As it was, my men were busy pursuing an anarchist assassin who was hiding in the US after a failed attempt on one of our leading citizens. I rely for my account of what took place on later conversations, supplemented by a photograph of the castle provided by a daring adventurer who was recording curiosities of Adirondack scenery at the time.

Prior to encountering that rancid body of water, they perceived the sulfuric stench of Lake Gaggamaggatt. The putrid, black lake was shrouded in mist, wisps and whirls seething up as though from a cauldron. Above their heads, a roof of ragged dark clouds signaled foul weather soon to come. They rode on in a bleak and eerie half-light.

"Whatever would prompt a man to build in such a wretched environment?" mused Holmes.

"It was not always thus," said Owl Eyes. "The place reflects its occupants."

The castle stood on a windswept height surrounded by terraces that may have once been landscaped but had become a jungle of wild brambles and scrub. The setting was ribboned with deep gullies. The forest had ended and there was naught but lichen and gnarly scrub bent and twisted by the wind.

In appearance the 'castle' appeared to be the work of local builders and masons based on stories they had heard, their actual experience with large structures confined to construction of factories, mills and the like. It might be called a fort more so than a castle.

There was a broad and towering main building of several stories, from which rambled attachments and annexes, topped with turrets and towers, looking as though an entire forest had gone into the construction. The main building displayed a few modest windows while the other structures were solid except for small hatches and peepholes. Years of harsh mountain weather had rendered all to a dark and gloomy patina.

Owl Eyes tied up the wagon and the pair proceeded on foot, creeping through the gullies so as to avoid observation, crawling as they worked their way toward the spot where the Indian said they would find a tunnel entrance.

Suddenly, on a rise above them, a tall figure in a dark cloak appeared. To the ordinary observer, the specter might have been terrifying. Holmes and Owl Eyes merely dodged behind a bush for cover.

"We have been spotted. It is Moran, coming out to meet us," Sherlock declared "Perhaps he has decided to have it out man to man, as did Moriarty."

A menacing figure cloaked in black, Moran stood peering in their direction. Sherlock stepped out from cover to confront his nemesis.

Moran then turned to one side to reveal a ferocious hound at his heels. "Attack!" he yelled.

The huge, snarling beast raced toward Sherlock, making a leap for his throat. As if reacting to an everyday occurrence, Sherlock seized the charging hound by its stout leather collar, turned, and, in an elegant move, swept it in arc high into the air. He released it on the downturn, sending the animal sprawling back toward its master.

"Keep your fool of a pet, Moran. You should know I am adept at handling hounds."

Shaking his fist and cursing, his opponent disappeared back into the castle.

"We dare not follow him directly," Sherlock said. "We could fall into an ambush. We must use the tunnel."

Moving cautiously and quietly, like a predator stalking prey, the Indian led him to an opening concealed behind bushes.

"You stand guard and I will have a look," Sherlock advised.

"You do not know the tunnel," whispered Owl Eyes.

"I am a quick study. This is my battle, my friend, you will be of greater help if you stay and sound a warning of trouble coming from this direction."

"So be it. Listen for the cry of the coyote, it is a sound that carries well."

The cobwebbed, dusty tunnel Sherlock followed led into a dark, dungeon-like basement area. As his eyes adjusted to the dim light, he beheld a strange image. There before him, in a cage, hunkered a wild-eyed prisoner. As the captive clutched at the bars and pulled himself up to full height, Holmes recognized him from reconnoiters around town. It was Rev Trogg.

"You are Sherlock Holmes and known to be a gentleman. Free me from this foul pit!"

Holmes stared at the prisoner for a long moment. "Where is Lillie?"

"McSnay took Mrs Langtry and fled." With a cunning smile he added: "I can help you find her if you let me out."

Holmes turned his back and spoke in the direction he had come. "I may. First explain why you are locked in."

"I will explain all, just let me out!"

"You will explain and I will then consider your plea. By my reckoning, your present quarters are suited to one of your character."

"McSnay did it. His predecessor, Moriarty, lured me into joining his network because he wanted the castle as a hideout for his minions on this continent. And so I became warden of a motley crew of outlaws. Then McSnay demanded I assist in obtaining Mrs Langtry's amulet. I secured the amulet but withheld it."

"Using it to lure Mrs Langtry to your disgusting den."

"Can you blame me? Have you ever seen such skin? Her skin is more lovely than the icing on a prize pastry."

Holmes strode to the cage and raised a finger in the face of the confined man. "You are a fiend, and madder than the sum total of inmates of Broadmoor. You killed Pettigrew for the amulet, and now you propose to skin poor Lillie in service of your mad hobby."

As this exchange was taking place, the room began to fill with smoke.

Owl Eyes emerged from the tunnel. "My grandson and his boys arrived and shots were fired at them, they have set the place afire with flaming arrows. I couldn't get to them in time to warn that you were within the walls. Hurry, it is going up fast."

"Tempting though it may be, I suppose I cannot let Trogg be roasted." Using a bar found nearby, Holmes forced the rusted door to the cell. "Where is Mrs Langtry? Tell me, or back you go."

Trogg, freed from captivity, seemed not to hear the question. He turned in the direction of the billowing smoke.

"My books! My dear, precious books!" With a hideous scream Trogg fled up a flaming staircase and disappeared into the conflagration.

Owl Eyes led the way out of the tunnel. "I have seen the one you call Moran and Mrs Langtry," he said. "They raced past me in a wagon, it appeared she was bound. Take care, all the inmates of this place are fleeing."

As they approached the wagon, a sinister-looking gang of half a dozen rogues from the castle surrounded them. "If it isn't the great detective," said one, a scar-faced brigand whom Holmes recognized from the London underworld. "We'll just have that wagon, thank you. Old man, you can head back to whatever cigar store you were decorating, it's your companion we want."

Owl Eyes loped off into the woods. Holmes, having found a stout stick to serve as a stave, battled members of the group trying to pull him from the wagon. He assumed Owl Eyes would return with reinforcements, his grandson and the young braves.

Chapter Nineteen

The gang, taking the worst of Sherlock's stave, blocked him in and made much of what they would do once he was in their clutches, some of the suggestions being frightfully disgusting.

"Take him alive! McSnay wants to see how he swims wearing cast-iron boots!"

A rumbling sound coming from the forest caught the attention of the assembly.

Suddenly, from the cover of the trees emerged a monstrous creature, an enormous bear. It was not the black bear common to the Adirondacks but a huge cousin, akin to the Kodiak of the far north. The enormous bear raised itself to full height on its rear legs and bellowed hideously, then, on all fours again, with growls that trembled the earth, made for the gang where they had stood discussing Sherlock's fate.

With screams and shouts, the crowd fled in all directions. A few random shots were fired but they seemed to pass through the great beast without his even noticing. The bear issued another mighty roar, looked at Sherlock, nodded and lumbered back into the woods.

Sherlock had remained standing on the wagon,

stave at the ready. The horse shifted and shied but bravely held his ground. Later, Holmes recalled: "In that monster I knew I had met my match. But his intentions toward me were apparently benign in nature; he was satisfied at having scattered my opponents."

In moments Owl Eyes reappeared and mounted the wagon. Sherlock studied him as they proceeded toward the place where they had left Watson and Yates. Owl Eyes maintained his gaze on the rough road ahead but seemed aware of Sherlock's observation. "Mirrors and smoke," the Indian muttered, without looking in the direction of his companion.

They found Watson standing guard over the prone Yates.

"He was awake for a while," said Watson, "muttering about the Society of the Golden Sun, something like that."

"Golden Dawn," said Holmes. "It is as I suspected. Mycroft had informed me that they had an agent in the area and asked for a report. It is a secretive group of intellectuals and literary sorts, apparently of no threat to society. This fellow, Yates, was assigned to retrieve a book stolen from their library. He was using his role as Mrs Langtry's butler as cover while seeking a way to access Trogg's collection."

"Do you refer to the bizarre book you had mentioned, the work of the madman de Sade?" asked

Watson.

"Yes. Trogg had secured the castle for his macabre library. Moriarty wanted the castle as a hideout. Moriarty used the de Sade book to bait Trogg into working with his group."

"Why the devil would Moran be involved with that sort of craziness?"

"Moran is now the leader of Moriarty's nefarious network and so had oversight of Trogg's operation at the castle. Trogg was assigned to obtain the purloined amulet from Pettigrew. For some reason they fought, no doubt over payment, and Pettigrew was killed. And then Trogg got it in his head to keep the amulet to lure Lillie into his clutches. Of course Moran was more than a match for Trogg's treachery, and now he has seized the amulet and abducted Lillie."

"We must rescue Mrs Langtry and recover the amulet," declared Watson.

"Yes, you have hit the nail on the head, Watson. However, you have driven that nail into nothing of substance."

"Meaning what, exactly, may I ask?"

"Meaning you have neglected a few minor details, such as their whereabouts, and how we shall accomplish this rescue."

"And you, meanwhile — perhaps in consultation with this Indian shaman — have divined the answers to both questions?"

Sherlock said the solution was not in divination but

in simple logic. That Moran had kept Mrs. Langtry as prisoner indicated that he thought she knew something about the treasure. That he was yet interested in the treasure indicated that he would remain in the general locality. But he could not be seen escorting a bound Lillie Langtry, so he must hide her somewhere. Where has he any privacy? The steam yacht.

"So, she is aboard the yacht. And how do we perform a rescue?"

"You, Watson, are the great fan of Stevenson, and so must be familiar with the tale of Treasure Island. We board the yacht like pirates, in the still of the night, swarming over the side."

"It is a small matter, Holmes, but my guess would be that the yacht will not be at the pier; rather it will anchored some distance out in the lake, for greater security. I suppose we shall swim out to it?"

"No, Watson, that is not my proposal. These Indians, you may have noticed, are possessed of a most remarkable small craft called a canoe. It slips through the water as silently as a floating leaf. We will ask Thibedeau for a canoe and get on with the rescue."

Watson wiped his hand across his forehead as though to erase an image from his mind. "I have seen those craft called canoes. Give me a good solid rowboat any day; the canoe looks a most precarious vessel."

"Not so, Watson. In times past, the odd one would float up on our home shores, meaning, as we were to learn, it had weathered the entire Atlantic. Such crafts are made with skills our own craftsmen can but envy. They are quite secure when handled properly, and silent, no creaking oarlocks."

"*If handled properly* … I mark those words, they may come back to haunt us."

"Calm yourself, Watson. You worry about every little thing. We will recruit Thibedeau to handle the canoe, you can lay back like the Queen of the Nile until called to action."

Yates was delivered to the Langtry mansion where he could rest and regain his health. The canoe was obtained from the encampment and, as darkness fell, the trio made for the lakeshore.

Chapter Twenty

In the dark by the pier, fishing boats and yachts rested in their berths, all was quiet. A slip of moon provided modest illumination.

"Are you cold?" Sherlock asked Watson. "There is no chill in the air."

"It's nothing. Just a bit of a shiver."

Thibedeau pushed the canoe into the water and held it secure. "Holmes, or Varner if you please, you will man the front with a paddle. Simply help to keep us in a straight course unless you hear me thump the side, one for left, two for right, three to revert to straight on. The doctor may take the middle. All he need do is remain still. We are not in current. There is a bit of breeze but no gusts, so the ride will not be unsteady if you maintain balance. They are anchored just offshore; we do not have far to go."

Sherlock moved easily to his position. The craft wobbled as Watson boarded. He waved his arms trying to regain balance. "I'm falling! I am going in!"

"Get a grip, Watson," commanded Holmes. "Once we are underway, if you go in, we all go in. It won't do."

Watson managed to bring himself to attention.

With care, he stepped to the middle and knelt down.

As if in a single move, Thibedeau pushed the canoe away from shore and swung himself aboard.

With only the slightest pat of sound, Holmes and Thibedeau guided the craft through the night. As the yacht loomed up ahead of them, visible by the dim light of the moon, Watson complained that he would not be able to keep his balance and climb the side of the yacht.

"Keep still," said Holmes. "Voices carry over water."

"So will the sound of my thrashing about when I tumble in," muttered Watson.

"Hush. There is a ladder."

Fortunately there was no one on deck to hear their voices. Thibedeau guided the canoe so that it brushed the side of the yacht, putting Holmes adjacent the ladder. "Wait until he puts you in position, Watson, then follow me."

After a bit of dramatic swaying and hesitation, Watson took hold of the ladder. Holmes helped him clamber aboard. "Now what?" whispered Watson.

"Listen!" hissed Holmes. From somewhere below they could hear rowdy voices of the crew. "The crew is deep in the whiskey barrel, as I suspected would be the case. My guess is Lillie will be imprisoned in the salon, just ahead of us. You are armed, of course?"

"Yes," Watson patted his chest. "The Webley that you provided is close at hand."

As they crept closer to the salon it became apparent that the party room was occupied. "We must be quick," Sherlock said. "We will burst in upon them, guns drawn, and free Lillie."

"As easily as that?" Watson glanced about furtively.

"The element of surprise is in our favor. Now!" So saying, he threw the entry door aside and stepped through, pistol at the ready. "Don't move, any one of you!" he ordered.

Then he noticed that Watson had not joined him. Reaching around the corner of the door he pulled the reluctant doctor into the room.

There were three men seated with Mrs Langtry at a card table. Two of the men were casually attired, distinguished by wide-brimmed western style hats, while one was decked out in gentlemanly finery. Given the moment when Sherlock was distracted, the two westerners rose up with pistols drawn while the third, recognized as Moran, fell to the ground and began slithering like a snake toward a rear door.

"You've ruined the game!" Mrs Langtry declared. To the two who had drawn their pistols she said: "Don't be alarmed. These are my friends Holmes and Watson. I suppose they have come to rescue me. It's all right; we weren't having much fun anyway. You boys claimed to know card games but you are very poor Whist players."

Meanwhile, Moran had made the rear door and

disappeared. "I do believe I have the pleasure of addressing Butch Cassidy and Harry Longabaugh, known as the Sundance Kid," Holmes said. "Your employer, Canfield, said we would find you aboard."

"At your service, then," said Cassidy. "We're all in favor of rescuing damsels in distress, although Mrs Langtry seems pretty much right at home."

"Surrounded by fire and brimstone, in the clutches of the demons," observed Holmes, "she would propose a tea party." He asked if they would busy the crew while he and Watson took Mrs Langtry to the canoe. "If you can impound the crew for a time, we will wait for you in the canoe we've brought."

"Will do. Even better, we know something about disabling steam engines; we'll slow them down but good. We would follow in the dinghy but, from the big splash I just heard, I'd say your adversary has gone with it."

"And taken the amulet with him, no doubt," said Holmes. "Well, we'll see to him later. If you fellows will be so kind as to attend to the crew, we will settle this lady in the canoe and await your return."

As they headed for the canoe, a great uproar arose below decks, several pistol shots rang out, and then all was quiet.

"You know," said Lillie, "that fellow Moran is really quite the gentleman. It was all rather exciting, being abducted. And then, once I had told him all I know about the treasure, he treated me as a guest."

"Such treatment would only last so long as it suited his purposes," said Holmes. "It is most exasperating, my dear woman; you are ruled by impulse rather than logic and fail to consider the consequences of your actions."

"I have not done badly thus far," Lillie huffed. She swung on to the ladder like a tomboy and descended to the canoe.

"There won't be room for all of us, or we will be too heavy for the boat," Watson muttered.

"You have no knowledge of the Indian canoe, Watson. That craft could hold ten of us, provided we kept our heads. Over you go, and be steady about it."

In moments the two cowboys had joined them. "The crew is tucked safely in the engine room," Sundance announced. "And it will be some while before that boiler is working again."

As the canoe glided toward shore, Holmes asked Lillie what she had told Moran about the treasure.

"I simply told him what I had read in Stevenson. It's not at all clear. He puts the expedition in the mountains over the course of several days. He says there were tall peaks in the distance, and they traversed a lowland forest across streams, an area strewn with boulders. They camped on high ground, overlooking a frozen lake."

"That could apply to a great many locales."

"So said Moran. And he said it was foolish to think that Stevenson would put the whereabouts of a treasure in a published book. But then he said he knew of an old Indian who had secret knowledge."

Sherlock said Moran must have been referring to Owl Eyes. "That puts our friend in grave danger, we must see to this safety."

"The yacht!" cried Watson. "It is moving toward us!"

By moonlight they could see the big boat bearing down in their direction. "They've gotten free and unfurled the sails," said Holmes.

"We should have chopped the masts. The sails are never used, we didn't think of it," said Cassidy. "We're sitting ducks if they start shooting."

"We may have to swim for it," said Holmes as he and Thibedeau put muscle into their paddling.

Just then, Thibedeau let out a ferocious yelp. "Hi-YEEEE!"

From the shoreline a barrage of flaming arrows flew in the direction of the yacht, some striking home. "My braves," said Thibedeau. "Now we will see who has to swim."

On shore, Sherlock proposed that they must make haste before the burning yacht attracted the authorities. He turned to Butch and Sundance. "Saracino is lurking somewhere hereabouts; it would be in your best interests to disappear quickly."

Cassidy nodded. "The yacht crew stables a few horses nearby. We'll take our wages out in horseflesh."

"Don't go too far," Lillie said to the cowboys. "Remember you promised to supply horses for my California ranch."

"Now," said Holmes, "it appears we have two buggies at our disposal. Watson, take one and escort Mrs Langtry to her estate. Thibedeau and I will take the other and try to reach Owl Eyes before Moran sets upon him."

"My boys will manage the canoe," said Thibedeau. "They know the back ways to the encampment."

"What if you are too late?" asked Watson. "What if Moran has seized Owl Eyes and gone for the treasure?"

"I am worried about my grandfather but I am told the treasure can protect itself. It is said the eye of Mad Bear guards the treasure. It has a hypnotic effect. The stone eye can drive a person mad if gazed at for any length of time."

"Yes," agreed Watson, "I have heard of such things occurring in India where jeweled statues protect temples. Of course, such tales are absolute nonsense."

Sherlock, an eyebrow arched, said he had read in the Norse sagas the report of a traveler to Vineland regarding a mystical red stone. "From the description, I would say it was a huge ruby."

"There are no rubies in this part of the world," Watson scoffed.

"Not so fast, Watson. As a matter of fact, there are

reports of a huge deposit near the southwest coast of Greenland. While it is in the form of a vein and must be dug out, portions have weathered out over the eons and could be picked up off the ground. Examples have been found among the native Inuit, and surely they would have traded or lost some to plunder. There was a report of one specimen the size of a grapefruit."

"I am not a geologist, Holmes. I defer to your expertise. And I believe we should get on with our tasks, I hear the bell of the fire apparatus."

Watson took the reins of a four-wheeler with Lillie at his side. As they passed through town, he suddenly reined in. "Look there, it is Moran talking with old Joe, the Indian. He is offering Joe a jug of whiskey."

"What can it mean?" asked Lillie.

"It is some sort of betrayal, you may be sure. Someone in old Joe's condition might trade his very soul for another drink. My bet is Moran was not speaking of our friend Owl Eyes but rather of Joe regarding the secret of the treasure."

"What shall we do?"

"We must keep an eye on Moran. If his dealing with Joe is as I suspect, he will lead us to the treasure."

"And I must have my beauty rest!"

"You can curl up with the lap rug. I don't know that you will get much rest, Moran will likely be taking rough roads, but we must pursue him. Surely it is worth your time for the opportunity to lay eyes on a ruby the size of a grapefruit."

"Drive on!"

Chapter Twenty-One

Moran, having secured a light horse-drawn wagon, led them a merry chase along back roads, climbing higher into the mountains. In all likelihood he was aware of being followed, but it did not appear to bother him in the least; he was obsessed with his mission, driving madly toward his goal.

The road narrowed and the ride became more jolting. "There is something familiar about this territory," Lillie said.

"Yes. We are heading toward the burnt-out castle. Our surroundings become more ominous the closer we get to it."

"Are we prepared to deal with Moran if the situation comes to that?"

"I have my Webley. My hope is that Sherlock will convince Owl Eyes to lead him in this direction, once it has been discovered that Moran pried the secret from old Joe."

Up ahead they saw that Moran had turned to a side lane.

"What is this? Moran is not going to the remains of the castle," said Watson, following their quarry to the rougher road, hardly more than a trail blazed through the shadowy forest. "Look ahead: What a grim, desolate bone-yard of a place!"

Moran had led them to the far side of the dismal lake. The best description of what they encountered came in a later note from Sherlock, in which he said it was "an exposed reef of ancient petrified fossils, once a seabed, now collapsed into a jumbled heap. Embedded in slabs of compacted sandy crust were ancient shark teeth, whale vertebrae, imprints of aquatic plants from ages past. There were numerous fissures and cracks in the surface layer leading to chambers, grottos, dark passageways beneath the surface."

They came upon Moran's buggy, hitched to the gnarled limb of a monstrous dead tree. "We must go on foot through this rubble," Watson said. He hitched their buggy and led the way through piles of huge slabs of ancient crust. "There is a path worn in the sandstone here."

The path led to a huge overhanging plate of rock covering the entrance to a shaft. "Moran has disappeared into this tunnel," Watson said. "We should wait here and hope that Sherlock follows soon."

"And let Moran have the treasure?" asked Lillie. "I think not. We must follow him."

Watson stood before her, arms across his chest. "No. It is too dangerous."

"You may stand guard if you wish. I am going in, I

want to see what he has found."

"I must insist that you stay."

"Insist to your heart's content, Watson. This will not be the first time insistence has been brushed aside by Lillie Langtry. I am going in." With set jaw and the determination of a charging lioness she pushed past Watson, whose feeble effort to block her path had no effect.

With nothing for Watson to do but follow, they crawled through a narrow opening and into a long passageway, tall enough to accommodate upright pedestrian traffic, coming at length to a great oaken door, fitted solidly into the rock.

Lillie examined the door: "You can see where the amulet fits it as a key. Unfortunately, we do not have an amulet. But I perceive that it is not necessary to unlock this door, someone has already done so."

Pushing through the door, they passed into an enormous domed chamber, dimly lit from fissures above, or perhaps some bioluminescent quality. It was of coliseum size and height, housing a vast, foul-smelling lagoon. The atmosphere was dank and sickly warm, as though the site had been enclosed for centuries –– which seemed entirely possible. "It is suited only to exploration by boat," said Watson, turning as if to make his way back to the entrance.

"There is a sort of path along the edge," Lillie replied, turning in the direction she indicated.

"It is too dark. We will need torches," Watson

observed.

"Your eyes will adjust. There is light from the fissures above, magnified by reflection from the lake and the white marble walls."

As their eyes adjusted they beheld an eerie scene. Along the narrow passageway between the lagoon and the ivory walls of the cavern were natural calcium or marble formations resembling all manner of strange creations – towers, steeples, hives, altars, eerie barricades.

Among the giant limestone statuary grew enormous mushrooms.

Lillie slowed to a cautious pace. "Watch your step, Watson. Beware of sinkholes and crevices."

"I'm more worried about sliding in this muck we are walking through."

"I recognize it from the studios of sculptors for whom I have posed," Lillie said. "It is the glacial clay used to make the famous Albany slip glaze, it can be as slick as glass."

"Heavens above, look at that!" declared Watson. Through the gloom they could see, on an outcropping jutting into the lagoon, a huge statue, somewhat aglow, or so appearing due to its composition. It stood five times the height of a man.

It was in the form of a gigantic bear.

Suddenly from beside them came a voice: "Welcome to the cave of Mad Bear! Watson, put that pistol of yours on the ground before I put you on the ground, thank you." Moran stood with a wicked looking sawed off shotgun aimed at the pair.

"What I want," said Moran, "is that ruby eye in the head of the bear. They say to gaze upon it is to go insane."

"Then you have us at a disadvantage," said Watson.

"How so?"

"You are already insane, it is as though you have been immunized."

"Ha, a fine joke. Well, how do like this for a joke? Watson, you must clamber up the side of that statue and prize loose the gem. Or else."

"Or else what, you villain?"

"Or else I will throw Lillie Langtry to the alligators."

"We are in the north country. There are no alligators."

Menacing him with the shotgun, Moran stepped forward and pulled the bowler hat from Watson's head, tossing it into the lagoon.

Huge jaws rose up and, with a violent snap, clenched the hat before disappearing back beneath the surface. "It may be as you say," said Moran with an evil smile, "but there is some beast here that does a very good imitation. So you will get on with it? Or shall we test the beast's appetite for British beauty?"

"There is no ladder."

"There are handholds at the side. Quit stalling,

unless you are eager to witness the gruesome demise of Lillie Langtry."

Watson strode to the base of the great statue and found the handholds. Looking up, he saw that the gem was emitting a pulsing light, as if warning of the incursion.

He began his ascent. As he climbed, the bear began to rock slightly.

"As I suspected," said Moran. "It is booby-trapped."

The bear began to sway precariously.

"I cannot hold on," Watson called.

"Climb, Watson, climb! The beast in the lagoon is hungry!"

Clinging to the handholds, Watson inched higher. As he neared his objective the statue twisted with some violence. He lost his foothold and dangled precariously, hanging on by his fingers. The statue lurched in the opposite direction, slamming him against it but allowing him to recover his footing. With as much effort put into simply holding on as to climbing, he at last reached the level of the bright red eye.

Now, the problem became one of retrieving the eye. Removing a pocketknife from his trouser pocket while holding tight with the other hand, he managed to open the knife.

With one hand, he pried at the gem. It popped loose and fell, to be caught by Moran waiting below.

"Release Mrs Langtry."

"Ha ha. You are a fool, and when that effigy crashes down you will be a dead fool! Enjoy your ride, Watson. Mrs Langtry, let us now see what sort of swimmer you are!"

At that moment a shot rang out and a giant stalactite crashed to earth just behind Moran.

He jumped forward, away from the shattering of the missile, but, in clutching to the ruby eye, lost his grip on the shotgun. It slid through the muck into the lagoon.

Butch Cassidy and The Sundance Kid raced forward toward Mrs Langtry as a cloud of calcite dust rose where the stalactite had crashed. With the dust cloud as cover, Moran dashed toward the entranceway, clutching his treasure to his chest.

Butch, Sundance and Mrs Langtry took up positions at the base of the swaying statue, ready to try to catch Watson if he should fall. But, with newfound vigor, Watson descended as nimbly as a monkey scrambling down a tree.

Just then, Moran came barreling back from the entranceway. "We're surrounded by bears!" he shouted, his eyes wide and wild.

As he passed, Watson tackled him. The ruby jumped from Moran's grasp and followed the path of the shotgun toward the edge of the lagoon. Moran broke free and bolted on down the path with Butch and Sundance in pursuit.

Watson leapt after the ruby, catching it just at water's edge.

Butch and Sundance returned. "Our boots are not cut out for traversing this slime," said Butch. "He got away, though he's gone deeper into the cavern. Who knows if there is another way out."

Sherlock, Owl Eyes and Thibedeau appeared at the entranceway. "Sorry for the delay," said Sherlock. "We had to convince Owl Eyes to show us the way."

"It's all right," said Lillie. "Doctor Watson performed admirably in your absence, saving me from a fate that included certain death in the jaws of a monster. He is a very brave man, and would make a better rodeo rider than our two cowboys together. No one has ever come to my defense with such passion."

Watson reddened as Lillie hugged him and kissed his cheek. "That is not quite the entire story," he said. "Really, it was Butch and Sundance who saved both of us. I am considerably in their debt."

"Is it safe to leave?" asked Lillie. "Moran said the entrance is surrounded by bears."

"Bears?" said Sherlock. "There are no bears, he ran at the sight of the three of us. He must have nibbled at these mushrooms."

"We have saved the eye," said Watson, "but what of the treasure? What of the Viking gold and silver plunder? Is it to be found deeper in the cavern?"

"Treasure, Watson? You are standing in its midst. Do you notice that this grotto abounds with huge mushrooms?" Holmes waved an arm at their surroundings. "These are giant Psylocibin mushrooms. Ingest a small dose and you may discover that you are a brother of Mad Bear, a ferocious combatant unrivalled in warfare. That was their treasure, the secret of the Berserkers' might, shared with their Bear Clan brothers. No, it is not gold and silver, but it is the wherewithal, the fuel that created savage warriors for whom the seizure of gold and silver was child's play."

"The gem that serves as sentinel for this place is, then, a thing best left to the keeping of the Guardians," said Watson, handing the glowing red ruby to Owl Eyes.

"Thank you," said the old shaman. "And perhaps some future generation will thank you. There may come a time when the ferocious powers represented by this gem are needed to combat a fanatical enemy."

As they departed the grotto, Sherlock stooped to retrieve a trinket abandoned by Moran in his lust to obtain the Eye of Mad Bear.

Chapter Twenty-Two

It was not many days before a great ceremony was held at the encampment, drawing Native Americans from throughout the region. Curious tourists and townspeople were welcomed as well, though they puzzled over the purpose.

Little was known of the meaning of an event described as the Festival of the Return of the Eye of Mad Bear. It was thought to refer to the activities of some secret Iroquois society, though not much thought was given to deciphering it as those outsiders present enjoyed the event.

It was a time for feasting. Tables were laden with foodstuffs: the traditional corn, beans and squash which are combined as a succotash as well as game meats, and a hearty supply of Thibedeau's increasingly popular chips of potato.

Mrs Langtry, in a moment when she was not being pestered by autograph seekers, suggested to Thibedeau that she might finance a venture producing the chips in bags for grocery sale. He greeted the prospect with eagerness and a date was set for further discussion.

A goodly crowd gathered to sample an array of

various berries such as strawberries, sweetened with maple sugar.

One arena featured the game of Lacrosse. "As a rough, fast-paced sport it is a cousin of Rugby," Watson observed.

In another arena, dancers in paint and feathers trotted and whirled, some wearing false face masks, accompanied by singers and tortoise shell or gourd rattles, bells and drums.

Elsewhere were other demonstrations of crafts and skills. Sherlock was invited to demonstrate his prowess at blindfolded archery but he demurred. "Your brave young lads need no competition for tourist bets."

Some visitors even listened to the ceremonial orations, though they were given in a language understood by few of those from the town. "Mostly, they are thanking the Great Spirit for this gathering and for the good things in our lives. Some are asking that the bad things be taken from us," Thibedeau explained.

"What sort of bad things?" asked Watson.

Thibedeau gazed off in the direction of town but made no response beyond a shrug.

Touring the tents to say their farewells at the conclusion of the event, Holmes, Watson and Mrs Langtry encountered Butch and Sundance engaged in a gambling game of bowl and beans. "We thought it best to lay low," Butch said. "Saracino and his pals are experts at mingling, no doubt they are represented in the crowd."

"I trust that when we next meet it will be at my California ranch," Lillie said.

"That may be easier said than done," replied Butch. "There is a lot of country for us to cross, and unfortunately the Pinkertons will be on watch all along the way."

"What you need is a diversion," suggested Watson.

"You have a suggestion?" asked Butch.

"I believe I have an idea," said Holmes.

Later, back at the boarding house, word came that Watson was released from suspicion in the death of Pettigrew.

"What of the amulet?" asked Watson.

"I have returned the amulet. It is back in Mrs Langtry's possession."

"But I must have it, I am on a mission."

"Do not concern yourself, Watson. It is her treasure, a gift from the future King of England. No doubt she will see that it goes where it belongs. I believe she intends to give it to Thibedeau in exchange for his cooperation in marketing those little slices of potato."

"But now Mycroft must report that I have failed. The Prince will learn that I did not recover the missing amulet. He might inform the Queen and I will be thrown in the Tower."

"The Queen has rooms full of treasure that she pays no mind to," scoffed Sherlock. "I cannot imagine she is even aware of the existence of the amulet."

"But that was the purpose of my trip, to retrieve it and save the Prince from having to admit his folly."

"The fact is, the Prince of Wales happens to owe me more than a few favors, so he agreed to conspire with Mycroft in creating a mission for you. We acted in the belief that a man with a desperate sense of mission may rise above the mire of addiction."

"Of all the … Holmes, this is unpardonable!"

"How can it be so, if it worked?"

"If I have failed to recover the amulet, how can you say your devious plot was successful?"

"Reflect upon events, Watson. You arrived on these shores in a muddled state, full of fantasies of doom and fears of any call to action. But quite recently you conducted yourself with genuine heroism. In addition to earning Lillie's undying gratitude, you will go down in Iroquois history as the man who saved the Eye of Mad Bear: the ultimate Guardian! There is no question of our success, though, much more importantly, your own."

The conversation was interrupted by the appearance of the Pinkerton man, Saracino. "I hear you fellows had an encounter with Butch and Sundance. Care to tell me where I might find them?"

Holmes shook his head. "No idea."

"You two are guests in this country. If you don't

want to cooperate, I might identify you as operatives of a foreign government."

Holmes turned to Watson. "You were the last to talk with them, as I recall. Did they give any indication of their plans?"

"I believe they were plotting a trip to South America."

Saracino gave Watson a piercing look. "South America! Now, there's a clever move. Are you certain?"

Watson nodded, his look one of absolute sincerity.

Saracino uttered an oath and hastily made for the door.

"Well done, Watson," said Holmes. "The Pinkertons will now be focused on the gateways to ocean travel rather than interior paths to California."

Epilogue

Having made their way to New York City, Holmes and Watson boarded a cruise ship ... bound for Argentina! They wore strange attire, the outfits of cowboys, from high-heeled boots right on up to broad-brimmed Stetson hats.

Holmes, studying his companion's gear, gave a snort, as near to a chuckle as was likely to come from him. "How are you adjusting to your new role, Sundance?"

"As well as you, I expect. Though, try as I might, it is going to be a real challenge to address you as ... Butch. And I must ask, is it essential that we wear plasters behind our knees?"

"They give us the gait of the cowboy, Watson, we must walk the walk as well as talk the talk."

Watson was quiet for a moment. "Do you suppose we are in violation of any law in this charade?"

"You imagine there is a statute of imitations?"

"Let us not give the lawmakers any ideas. By the way, what in the world will we do in Argentina ... Butch?"

"Nothing. We will leave Argentina to those who follow us. Via Mycroft, arrangements have been made to meet up with a British warship coming from the Falklands, we will transfer to it in secret. And Saracino will arrive in Argentina to learn that the cowboys have simply disappeared. Surely that will satisfy your debt to the real Butch and Sundance."

"Indeed so. And what of Moran?"

"On the off chance that he survived the encounter in the cave of Mad Bear, he will learn through his criminal connections that our friends Butch and Sundance are alive and well; rumor will have it they are headed back to the wild American west and their outlaw escapades. It will then dawn on him that you and I are the ones who sailed to Argentina. As he is still bent on avenging Moriarty's demise, he will be off after us, likely to spend a year or two chasing phantoms on the Pampas. In that time I shall dismantle his London connections, he will be without resources upon his return."

"You are talking very British … Butch. Talk western, we're now cowboys."

"Very well. I am open to lessons."

"As a matter of fact, I happen to have learned a very cryptic cowboy phrase."

"And do you intend to share your knowledge?"

"I believe it is a term of affirmation. I asked if they thought you and I could successfully impersonate a pair of outlaws. As one voice, they replied, *Shoot a raccoon.*"

"I wonder if you got it quite right?"

Watson bristled. "I suppose you have a better idea of what was said?"

"Shoot, I reckon."

The End